COVEN COVE

Blood Wars

David Clark

1

"I don't understand how any of this will help."

I thew my arms up, making my aggravation clear. They fell back down and slapped the top of the table. The impact echoed throughout the library. Of all the places she could have picked, Mrs. Saxon chose this one to add to my house arrest. Not the pool. Not the woods. Not the cove. The library. All because no one ever visited here. If they needed something, they summoned Edward to their room, or wherever they were. It wasn't like anyone would question a locked library door. Not that anyone would try to open it.

"You have been through a lot, and Mrs. Saxon believes that talking to someone about it might help," replied Edward from the spot his head hovered over.

"I don't need therapy!" I pounded the table with each word.

"Of course not, and I'm not a therapist. Do you see a couch anywhere? Am I sitting on a leather chair with my legs crossed and a pad of paper sitting on my lap ready to take notes with?"

"No. I don't see a couch, and I don't," I paused and looked away from Edward before I pointed out the obvious. My hand motioned to the space under him, "and I don't see any legs."

"Touché Miss Dubois. Touché." He circled around in front of me and looked me in the eye.

I felt embarrassed at my comment; It was a childish joke born out of the frustration of this, our third pointless session. "I'm sorry." I looked up at him sheepishly.

"It's no worry, Miss Dubois. Emotional stress often causes people to lash out. Now, shall we continue?"

"Sure," I agreed. Not that I had a choice. "Where were we?"

"The same place we started two days ago, Nathan, and how his turning into a vampire made you feel. Let's start there, please."

He was right. That was the first question he asked me during our first session, and the same question he had asked me several dozen times since. All I did each time was deflect. I believed that was a term a therapist would use, though Edward never did. Why there? Despite asking multiple times across multiple visits, including now, I still didn't understand. It was time to ask again. "Why do we need to start there?"

"Do we have to go through this again, Miss Dubois?"

If he was going to ask that question again, then yes, we would have to go through this again. This time I held my tongue, and propped my head on my arms, and prepared myself for Edward's answer. It had been the same answer for the last two sessions. I was sure it would be the same this time, too. Edward didn't disappoint.

"Miss Dubois, you have been through a traumatic event. Talking to someone could be beneficial, and as Mrs. Saxon and most of the others here in the coven are emotionally invested, I'm the best option. Not to mention I am a good listener. I am mostly ears." His head twisted back and forth, displaying the ears on either side of his floating head. "Beyond that, you need to bring your emotions in check if you are to continue with your training. Might I ask how that is going?"

My arms collapsed on the tabletop, along with my head. "Miserable," I said. The table muffled my voice.

Nothing was working. Not even a flash or flicker. Several of my old standbys, the things I could do as a young girl, were no shows. Telekinesis was one of my earliest discoveries, and now poof, it had vanished.

I didn't doubt Edward on his theory about the connection between my emotional state and my magic. I had even tried to address it on my own last night by attempting some meditation. That was something James had mentioned as a method of clearing my mind during my divination training in the witch's camp. It cleared my mind. That was for sure. It created a lot of room for thoughts of Nathan to come crashing in. All that did was send me into an emotional tailspin. The more I thought of him, the emptier I felt. A true and tragic irony. My head would be full of thoughts of him, but that empty feeling hole his absence created grew larger.

"Let's identify what it takes to put you back on track. Shall we?"

My head nodded against my arms, and then I sat up. "I don't disagree, but maybe we are focusing on the wrong starting place."

"Why do you think that?" he asked presumptuously.

Oh, how very therapist-like of him.

I needed to prepare myself. Once we got into this, there would be a bunch of and-why-do-you-feel-that-way questions, and I would have to tell him. If I'm being forced to endure this, then I need to get something constructive out of it. Didn't I? Mrs. Saxon gave no indications she would drop this idea soon, and my magic was a mess. There was no way to avoid it. "I was fine when Nathan changed. I mean... Was I upset when it happened? Yes. I was devastated. Why wouldn't I be? The man I loved died trying to save me."

I held up a finger to stop Edward from stating the obvious.

"I know. I know. He didn't die, but you know what I mean. But I could still function. My magic was on point. Even stronger than before. Wouldn't the troubles have started then if that was the reason?"

Edward looked away and then floated around the room and back. Then he did it again. It was almost as if I could see a body underneath his head pacing while his arms and hands rubbed his chin in thought. "It's possible. Though your emotions could have driven your magic to continue, like a shot of adrenaline that kept you going following a traumatic event."

"Is that even possible?" I wondered out loud. "I mean, I know what you are talking about. Or let me correct that. I remember what you are talking about. That burst of energy that keeps you going even when you are exhausted." I remembered it clearly from my youth. We woke up one night to a fire in our fields. We never figured out how it started. All I remember was hearing my father screaming to wake up his farm hands at a little after three in the morning. The exhaustion I felt when I went to bed just hours before was gone. I was up, alert, and running to the field to help shovel dirt on top of the approaching flames. We worked well into the next day without stopping. I felt my exhaustion set in once the flames were out, but not before. I was driven and energized the whole time.

"But does that exist for magic? And" I stood up from the table. "Would that last for several days? I was doing quite well during my training down there. There wasn't even a hint of a problem. Not until... I returned after..." That was it. It hit me like a bolt of lightning. I didn't even know why this was a mystery. That moment was so painfully etched into my memory, I couldn't even speak of it. I couldn't say it out loud. That was the moment everything went on the fritz. It wasn't immediate, but the first small failings started then.

"The moment he refused to come back with you. Yes, I am well aware of the proximity of that event to the start of your problems, but in my experience," Edward rotated around to face me. "Which is considerable when you consider how many years I have been around, and all the generations of witches that have come through my doors. It is never that simple. Therefore, I think we need to go back. So, humor me." Edward rose a few feet and looked down his nose at me. "How did you feel when Nathan turned?"

And here we were again. We were stuck in this vicious cycle. I actually thought we were on to something this time. Yes, Edward had a point. I was falling into the trap of a simple causality. Because one thing happened after another, then it must have caused it, but in this case I felt it really did cause it.

"I just told you," I said with a shake of my head. I wasn't sure why we were going back through this, considering I just bared my soul to him about that moment.

"What a little bitch," exploded Mrs. Saxon as she entered through the formerly locked library doors.

Hearing that tone, and that term, from her put me on the defense and I backed up into a table, pushing it and its chairs back a few noisy feet. "I'm sorry," I said, and readied myself to fall to the floor and beg for her forgiveness. She must have been watching us all this time. I knew that the warm welcome I received when I returned wouldn't last forever. How long it had lasted already had me amazed.

"Oh no. Not you, Larissa," apologized Mrs. Saxon. Visibly frustrated and flustered. "That little..."

"Witch?" I interjected, to save her from the other word I felt was on her lips.

"Yes, witch. Thank you, Larissa. That little witch Miss Sarah Roberts."

I second guessed my choice of correction. I should have let Mrs. Saxon stay with her original term.

"Every time I try to ask Mrs. Wintercrest about what happened in New Orleans, and the rumored attack on the vampires, Miss Roberts steps in between us and turns it around. Then she questions my motives now that my son is a vampire. What gives her the right?"

"She is a council member."

"Thanks for pointing that out, Edward. It's not like I didn't already know that," sniped back Mrs. Saxon. She walked up to the closest table and pulled out a chair and collapsed into it. "I'm sorry Edward."

"No apology needed, ma'am."

"No, I am sorry. It's not you, it's them," she huffed. "They aren't even trying to lie or deny things. Every time I direct the question at our supreme, she just stands there and smiles while someone else steps in and deflects it. Never answering the question at all. Not even with a lie, which any attempt to deny it is happening would be at this point."

"Is happening?" I asked for a clarification that I hoped was just a poor choice of words by Mrs. Saxon. Not that she made that kind of mistake often. She was a proper person when she spoke.

"Yes, Larissa. Is happening. What happened wasn't isolated to New Orleans, and it is continuing. Jen and Kevin are hearing from others about isolated attacks on some of the smaller vampire covens. Most are those that are just a single-family unit or a few families together, but that doesn't matter. It is happening, and it shouldn't be.

"What about New Orleans?" I asked as I rushed over and took the chair next to her.

"I don't believe there has been another attack since the last one, but I don't know for sure."

"There has to be someone we can talk to. Someone that can stand up to the council and put a stop to this." I pounded the table to add an exclamation point. It echoed through the cavernous library. I couldn't believe this was happening. Witches. The council at that. They were openly attacking vampires, but why? That was a stupid question. I knew why. Nathan had already told me, and he was right. They were different, and a potential threat to the witches, like how they viewed me, and now that Jean was gone, sort of, and Marteggo was definitely gone, there was an opening, and no one to stand in their way, but that is too simple. It explained what happened in New Orleans. Jean and his coven were a problem, and so were the rogue witches. An opportune time to solve two problems. That didn't explain what they were doing now.

"There used to be. That was Master Thomas," responded Mrs. Saxon. "But not now, and I'm afraid it is too risky to approach anyone else."

"What about Mr. Nevers?" I spouted, remembering his constant presence during my training here and again in New Orleans.

"Not even him, I'm afraid." She walked over to the table that I pounded in protest. "I don't doubt he would listen to us, but what could he really do?"

Nothing. That was what he could do. I knew it, and approaching him would be a onetime thing. The moment he spoke out against anything that was going on in the council, they would likely kick him out. Just like they had with Master Thomas. This was hopeless, and I felt it as I collapsed down on the table.

"Larissa." I heard the legs of the chair beside me squeak on the floor as Mrs. Saxon slid it out and sat. "I don't want this to sound like I am putting more pressure on you, but really, our only way out of all this is to complete your training, and then challenge for supreme." Her hand reached over and stroked the top of my head.

Nope, she wasn't adding any pressure on top of me. Nope, not at all. She was only laying all the pressure in the world on me. It sounded so simple when she said it. It was way too simple, and yet, she was right. It would solve everything. I looked up. "How exactly can I do that? Challenge for supreme? I am a fugitive that escaped from a prison they sent me to for crimes against all witches... oh wait, they labeled me a hostile entity. I seriously doubt I can walk right up and make the request."

"Well," started Mrs. Saxon, and then I saw something I had never seen from her the whole time I had known her. Her eyes darted around the room and avoided mine. Even her body language changed. There was a slight slump in her shoulders, and a small slow exhale before she finished her answer. "I'm still working on that." Then there was a lengthy pause. I looked up at Edward, who hovered above the center of the table. He was also waiting for a further reply from Mrs. Saxon. This was a pretty significant step in the plan. Hearing she was still working on it was disheartening.

"Under normal circumstances, any witch can approach the council and request permission to take the test of the seven wonders," she continued.

"Well, these are most certainly not normal circumstances." That was the understatement of eternity. "But say, these were, and I wasn't me. Then what? How does it normally work? Just because I can perform them, I replace the supreme?"

That had been a question in my head for a few days now. Lisa could do some, if not all, of the wonders. I was sure there were other witches out there that could. The fact that I can, and Mrs. Wintercrest can, means at least two witches can perform all seven. Who decides who is supreme then?

"It's not that straightforward."

"It never is." Edward's remark earned him an admonishing look from Mrs. Saxon.

She straightened up and turned toward me. "There are two paths. One, if you show greater ability than the current supreme, then the appointment as supreme is automatic and unchallenged. I believe that is your path to becoming the supreme. Mrs. Wintercrest is aging, and as a witch ages, some abilities become diminished. Now if there is no discernible difference between the two witches. It becomes the choice of the council where they are to take other factors into consideration. They would consider the person, their deeds, and how they would benefit our community."

I looked right up at Edward. "So, a popularity contest."

He nodded.

"Well, I ain't winning one of those with that group anytime soon."

"I don't disagree, which is why your training is so important."

"Yep," I conceded. What else could I do?

"On that topic, any major breakthroughs?"

"Well, ma'am, today I believe Larissa fully embraced our sessions, and I believe we will..."

Mrs. Saxon raised a hand, cutting off Edward. "That is fine, and an important part of her journey, but I am more curious about her magic. Larissa, how is that going? Any improvement since yesterday?"

"Not really. It's still inconsistent."

"How inconsistent?"

I had hoped she hadn't picked up on my choice of words there. Inconsistent was really stretching it. "Basically, not there at all. What does come is a surprise."

"Not good. Not good at all," Mrs. Saxon said as she stood up from the table. "It's all the turmoil in your world. You need to put all that back into order for everything else to fall in line."

"I know." I honestly did. It made complete sense to me. That word I hated so much, focus, described exactly what was absent from my life.

"I hate to do this, but we need to double your sessions. You will meet with Edward twice a day. Once down here, and again in your room. We can't risk anyone walking in after classes and seeing you in here."

I held my scoff inside. No one would ever come in here.

"We will also double your sessions with Master Thomas and myself. Mornings before my first classes, and then evenings. In the meantime, I will talk to Mrs. Tenderschott about a potion to help you. It won't be a cure. Just a temporary solution so you can train. You won't be able to use a potion or anything during the seven wonders. They'll know."

"Okay." What else could I do other than agree, no matter how much I didn't want to do the double sessions? I didn't mind the training, but this therapy session was out-and-out torture, and one big reminder of everything that was going wrong. I didn't need any reminders of that.

"Head on up. I will be up shortly." Mrs. Saxon turned and spun her hand, opening a portal up to my room. It had barely materialized before Samantha ran through the portal and wrapped her arms around my legs. Then the one-month-old who was going on five years old hopped up on her grandmother's lap while giving Edward a rather cautious wave.

"You need to remember who you are fighting for. It's not you, me, Master Thomas, or anyone like that." Mrs. Saxon stroked Samantha's auburn hair as she said it.

2

"Please!" I begged, not being shy about how desperate I sounded. Not that I liked how it sounded, but I needed Master Thomas, Marie, or anyone else sitting around me to hear the anguish I felt.

Master Thomas threw his arms out and twirled around. A cold winter gust swept through the open space, sending the hem of his overcoat floating up around him. I didn't share the same enthusiasm, and ran my hand across my face.

"I got you out. See? Convincing Rebecca to allow this took a while." He gestured towards the barren trees around the clearing. Winter had long ago stolen their foliage. He was right. It took a week of him talking to Mrs. Saxon for her to grant what Master Thomas called small, supervised-field-trips to the woods. He suggested that Samantha should experience more of the world. It seems, while Mrs. Saxon found it easy to deny me, she found it harder to deny her granddaughter. He also gained permission to include Marie Norton and Jen Bolden. He sold them as chaperones who weren't witches and wouldn't be able to whisk me away someplace.

He was rather proud of his accomplishment and didn't quite understand the disappointment that sent me running to my bed when he first told me. This wasn't what I had in mind when I said I wanted to leave. I wanted his help to go find Nathan. A feat that if I could, I would have already done it for myself, but I couldn't, so I hadn't. He ignored the dozens of plans I told him about how I would convince Nathan to return with us.

"You know what I meant," I complained.

"Of course I do, and you know as well as I do, that is completely out of the question. That is also why there are no other witches as part of your little escapades. Just me. And I'm not about to open any portals to any place but back to your room."

"Sam is a witch," I remarked, just to remind him.

"Yes, she is, but she is... too young to open a portal."

"You tried to pick an age, didn't you?" I teased after hearing him stumble in the middle of his statement. I looked back at my beautiful daughter as she ran back and forth between Marie and Jen, giggling the whole time.

"I tried, but I am not sure. That is something beyond my comprehension."

"Something you don't understand?" I quipped, enjoying the chance to needle him a little.

"This is one of the many things in the world that I don't understand. She looks between four or five, but I know she's not."

"That's my guess too. Just going based on how she looks and acts." I looked at him eagerly and asked, "So, when do we start her training?" I wasn't sure who that question caught more off guard. Me or Master Thomas. I felt his heart skip while I wondered to myself why I had even asked that question. The more I considered it, the more it became a valid question. A very valid question.

"Let's focus on getting you back to training first," he replied.

"I wasn't much older than Sam when I started. I think I was six."

Master Thomas's tone turned stern, and he turned to look right at me. "As much as you ask me to help you find Nathan, or to help stop what is going you, recovering your own abilities and your own training should be your focus. That is the only path to what you seek."

"I know. That's what Mrs. Saxon said too."

"You need to remember that and stay focused." He paused and looked at Samantha. "But yes," his tone softer and friendlier. He sounded like the Master Thomas I remembered, with a touch of curiosity. "She looks and acts like a six-year-old. That is usually the age when formal training starts. We don't know what her true age is. She may really only be a one-month-old. It is one of many things we don't know." Master Thomas hesitated and extended a hand toward Samantha. "I mean, we don't even know what she is."

"What the hell?" I huffed. "She's a child. My child. What do you mean we don't know what she is?"

"Exactly." Master Thomas glanced in my direction.

I wasn't sure if he was being funny or serious. Either way, it burned.

"We know she is at least part witch. That much is sure, and like her mother, she is primarily a telekinetic."

Just two weeks ago we gave her the test all young witches go through. I stood there a nervous and anxious mother, watching my daughter grab hold of that crystal. When I saw the same brilliant blue light that I had seen just several months ago, I fought the urge to cheer. I don't remember going through a similar test when I was younger, but perhaps I did when I was her age and was just too young to remember.

"So, what else is there to know?" I asked, not knowing where he was headed with this. The question was always was would she be a witch or not? Now we had our answer.

"Whether she has any vampire in her?" Master Thomas stated flatly, standing facing me with his hands clasped in front of him.

Wow. I could honestly say I wasn't prepared to hear that. That thought had never occurred to me. Why would it? She breathes. I feel the warmth of her breath against my cheek when I snuggle with her at night as she sleeps. Which is another thing. She sleeps. Let's not forget about how she shivers when she feels my icy touch. Something I had learned to mask with lots of blankets. Her heart beats. Something we had all felt. Mrs. Saxon even had to put up a block around my room to keep the other vampires from sensing her as they passed up and down the hallway. Blood flowed through her body, giving her cheeks that wonderful rosy complexion. Something her mother no longer had naturally. "She's human. That's plain to see."

"Is it?" Master Thomas asked while again giving me a side glance.

"Absolutely," I responded, almost a little defensive.

"Yes, she has a heartbeat, and appears human, but take her growth rate. That is more than a little accelerated, and I don't believe we can chalk it up to any of the magic that may have contributed to her being here."

"Why not?"

"It's quite simple." Master Thomas turned and addressed me directly. "The same reason the baby duck appeared when you thought about it. If you had thought about a child at a certain age, they would have appeared at that age. If magic were at play in Samantha's conception, then you imagined having a baby with Nathan. It's a logical understanding and progression of facts. Her progressive aging is something else."

"You're right," spouted Marie, as Samantha collapsed into her arms. She wiggled as Marie attempted to hold on to her before finally letting her go race toward Jen.

"Well, don't keep us in suspense."

"Yes, Marie, do tell," I prompted curiously. I wasn't even aware she was listening to us. Our conversation wasn't exactly private, but she appeared occupied with Samantha.

"You're right. It is something else." She stood up as Samantha returned to crash into her. This time she crashed into her legs, laughing. Marie reached down and rubbed her head before she sent her off toward Jen, who full on tackled her and started tickling her, causing an eruption of laughter. "I'm, I mean we—Jen and I–, aren't saying she is a vampire, but Larissa, do you remember Theodora saying vampire pregnancies were faster than those of humans?"

I rolled my eyes. How could I forget that? She said it all the time, and I lived it. Man, did I live it.

"While you and Sam are completely unique, births to a vampire male and human woman are rare, but they happen."

"The Dhampirs that Theodora mentioned?" I interjected.

"Yes, Dhampirs. Those pregnancies usually last for only a few months. Much shorter than a normal human pregnancy, but it doesn't stop there. Once born, the child ages faster than a normal human child would. How fast is different for everyone. Some I have heard of age quickly through the first few months. Then they reach an age when everything returns to normal. It's usually at a really young age.

Maybe five or six. Those children are pure human. There are those who reach an age and stop aging completely. They inherit some of the vampire traits from their father. Immortality. Their speed and strength. Their enhanced senses. Even their ability to consume blood. Who's to say that..."

Three sets of eyes looked in Samantha's direction, finishing the question Marie had started. Was it possible? The roles were reversed here. Did she inherit more from me than just being a witch? How the hell could we find out? "I am guessing there isn't a crystal we can have her hold?"

"No," laughed Marie.

"We just have to watch her," said Jen. "See if she shows anything on her own."

"Wow," I said, and walked over to a stump to have a seat. "I never considered the possibility she could be both."

"You may not be the only one anymore," remarked Master Thomas.

I was unsure how to feel about that. It had nothing to do with losing that unique distinction of being the only one. That was something I couldn't have cared less about. I just didn't want her to have to go through what I was going through.

Dang it! Another life screwed up by me, and another life that hung in the balance of everything I had to take care of. Not that Samantha's didn't already rely on me completing this greater task that Master Thomas, and I guess Mrs. Saxon, had assigned me. Everyone was relying on me. But if Samantha were both, now she was part of the Jean problem. If Jean ever found out there was another one like me, I already knew what he would do.

"I cursed her." I thought I had whispered it, but I obviously hadn't. Everyone, including Samantha, looked over at me.

"What is it mommy?" Samantha cried as she ran in to my direction.

"Oh, nothing," I said, brushing the hair back out of my eyes before she arrived. Then I reached down and picked her up onto my lap. "Nothing. Mommy is just being silly. She does that from time to time."

"It's about time she realized it too," remarked Jen.

I stuck my tongue out in her direction. Samantha did the same, but she was more enthusiastic about it than I was.

Master Thomas motioned for me to make space for him on the dead tree trunk I sat on. I did, and he sat down. Until he sat next to me, rigid back, and all, I hadn't realized I was slouching. Since when had I started doing that without having to force it? Maybe that was a good thing.

"Now, she is what she is. We'll have to wait to find out what she really is. I will start her training as a witch. You, on the other hand, know what you are, and we must return you to that. This is your afternoon training session. Let's get started."

"Do we pick up where we left off this morning?" I asked, knowing that it didn't really matter. This morning's session was just Master Thomas working through a litany of various spells and hand magic. As we went spell by spell, he provided an example, and then asked me to perform them. These sessions irked me more than a little. I knew each of these spells, and had performed most of them a couple of hundred times in my life. I knew how. That wasn't the problem. It was my performance that was lacking.

"No, let's start back at the beginning, with what comes naturally to you. Once you can control that, we will build upon that foundation."

With a little pat on the bottom, Samantha went back to Jen and Marie to have fun. I needed to return to my misery.

We had already tried this several times this morning. Each time, Master Thomas floated something in front of me and asked me to push it away. Each time I couldn't. This afternoon was no different. This time it was a dead branch with three lonely dead leaves clinging to it, not that there were many other options out there in the woods on a winter day. The cold winter winds had blown away most of the leaves and left the ground barren

I went back to basics, or what Master Thomas called basics, and closed my eyes. In my head, I imagined the object he held in front of me, the branch. I could see it clearly. That was never the problem. I even felt it. That wasn't the problem either. I could even feel the surrounding universe. That wasn't a problem anymore. It was at first, but not now. The problem was that the universe was a huge, knotted ball of string. The harder I tried to make sense of it, the worse it got. Like a demonic Rubik's cube that reshuffled itself when you were close to solving it, not that I was close to solving anything.

For this test, I didn't need to make complete sense of it. I just needed to imagine a wind projecting out away from me and pushing the branch. I focused, a term and state I had loathed, but now I knew was necessary.

"See the branch, Larissa," prompted Master Thomas.

"I do."

"Now, project out."

I squeezed my eyes harder, as if that would help, and I even felt my hand give a little shove forward, but I sensed nothing coming out. When I opened my eyes, I wasn't surprised to find nothing had moved. The dead leaves still dangled on the branch. They were taunting me. Maybe I should imagine the leaves are Jack, or better yet, Gwen.

"I need a booster shot," I mumbled at the sight.

"You need a what?"

I shook my head, disheartened by another failure, and explained weakly. "James, in the witches' camp, pushed me hard on the forehead when I had a problem focusing during his lesson on divination. It worked and brought everything into focus."

"Huh?" Master Thomas wondered aloud.

"I can see it, but... I don't know. The world around seems to be in so much chaos I can't even do the simple things that don't require me to pull on any of the strings. I can understand why the hard things being a problem, but the simple ones?" An involuntary huff escaped out from my mouth.

"Huh?" Master Thomas repeated.

"I mean, this is stuff I was doing long before you explained how to reshape the fabric of the universe to create new magic."

"Huh?" He repeated it for a third time, and this time I jerked around and looked right at the side of his face with an intensity that could have cut a diamond.

"Will you stop saying that?" I barked. "What is it?"

"Your booster shot idea," he said, as if he was questioning himself. "That might be a possibility here." Then he finally turned and regarded me, adding me to the conversation. "It is possible. Think of it as a more forceful form of consumption. We might be able to clear some of the clutter away, and you could..."

I reached over and grabbed him by the shoulders and screamed. "Do it now!" Then I closed my eyes and leaned my head toward him to give him a clear shot at my forehead. I wanted to feel his thumb's thump, like I had with James. All I felt was Master Thomas removing my hands off of his shoulders and placing them back down on my lap.

"Larissa, I am afraid that's not the solution to our problems. That will only clear the confusion in your head temporarily. It won't unravel that chaos that surrounds you. You may be able to do simple hand magic and some spells, but nothing complex and you absolutely won't be able to train for the test of the seven wonders. Not until we unravel things."

I felt what little hope I had inside shrink. I should have known it wasn't that easy. Nothing in the world of witches was. Make that nothing in my world was, but my mind hung on to a small piece of what Master Thomas had explained. "How long would it last? If you were to do it?"

"A moment. Maybe a few minutes to an hour," he shrugged. "It's hard to know. It depends on you and what is on your mind. Which it would help to know–"

"Don't start analyzing me," I interrupted. "Edward does enough of that as it is." I glanced over at Samantha playing with Marie and Jen. "It's not like it is any big mystery," I muttered.

"No, it's not. At least not to me. But we have to find a way to clear it, or you won't be able to address it."

"Thank you, captain obvious for pointing out the universe's catch-22." Realizing I snapped at my mentor, I jerked up straight and turned to him. "I'm sorry."

Master Thomas brushed it off with a smile. "It's all right. I've been waiting to hear a little of the old Larissa slip out. Maybe that would help, but," and he held up a hand to block any attempt I made to interrupt him, "if you want to talk about it, you can talk to me. I am a good listener, and I was there with you, so I would understand more than Edward or Mrs. Saxon may. It's just an offer, not a command."

I accepted it with a sheepish nod. I knew he meant well, and he was right. They all were. I was tired of being surrounded by so many people who seemed to know how to run my life better than I did. What made it even worse is they were right. But, it wasn't as simple as "do step a," and then "do step b", followed by "step c". I knew what my problem was. It was Nathan, and that ache I felt inside every time I looked at Samantha. His absence had created a hole that grew with every thought, and knowing about the war just multiplied the sense of dread I felt.

I used to feel guilty for hoping the vampires got a few shots in at the witches, but no longer. Well, that wasn't exactly true. I still felt guilty, and I hoped there weren't witches blindly following the orders of their council. Those were the ones I felt for. The ones that knew full well what they were doing were the ones that I hoped got what they deserved.

"Can we try?" I asked politely. "Even if it is just for a few minutes." I watched Master Thomas' face contort and twist as he considered my request. I needed to give my case a little booster to push him further to my side. "Perhaps feeling things flowing again would lead to better clarity."

"All right," he agreed reluctantly. "There may be potions that would extend things. Mrs. Tenderschott should be our next stop, but here goes nothing." James had used his thumb against my forehead, but Master Thomas gripped my head at the temples and boom. There it was, that wonderful nothingness. The lines of the universe were still the biggest knot I had ever seen, but inside, there was a section of nothingness. A spot not occupied by my larger task, or worry about Nathan, or schemes of how to put my family together, well not exactly. If I could find a way to make this clarity last longer, this might open a few doors.

"Now. The branch."

I didn't have to close my eyes this time. I saw it, I felt it, and better yet, I felt a force projecting outward from me. It wasn't as strong as before, but it clearly moved the dead leaves that dangled from the branch he levitated in front of me.

"Come on, you can do better than that," challenged Master Thomas.

"I wasn't trying. I just wanted to see if I could move anything."

"Really focus Larissa. See the branch. Feel its presence. Feel the energy surging inside you and project out. Push with your hands if you need to."

The way he treated me as a novice witch grated on my nerves. Determined to silence his doubts, I gracefully released a single leaf, sending it soaring high into the stratosphere. In that moment, I displayed not only raw power, but also an undeniable mastery over my abilities. I was proud of myself, and I had hoped he would be too. If he was, he didn't say anything. He didn't have a chance before another force sped past both of us and knocked the branch halfway across the clearing. We looked back toward its source and saw Marie and Jen with their hands over their mouths, and Samantha with her arms outstretched.

3

"Let's go. You're mine for a bit." Mrs. Tenderschott called through the spinning portal that just appeared in my room.

"But I'm not supposed to leave my room except for my sessions in the library." I pointed down at the floor to emphasize my point and left my Master Thomas chaperoned field trips out of it. I wasn't sure if they were public knowledge yet.

"Since when did you follow rules?" Lisa asked, poking her head through the open portal. Then she looked beside me and stumbled through the portal. "That can't be."

Samantha shuffled behind me to hide. She is not a shy child, though she hasn't really been around many people before, and definitely not someone that looked like Lisa.

"Jack," she called, and another familiar head poked through. He looked more stunned than Lisa as he stepped through.

Lisa stumbled a few more steps before she kneeled in front of me and peered around my legs to meet Samantha eye to eye. "She's precious."

"She's so b-b-big."

Lisa and I both gave Jack an annoyed look. Lisa turned her attention back to Samantha, holding out her hand. "I'm Lisa, a friend of your mom's."

"Sam," I said, looking down at the cowering girl. Her eyes were about to burst. I reached my hand down and rubbed the top of her head, and encouraged her to move away from her make-shift shield. "This is Lisa and Jack. They are both witches. They are both very nice." I winked at Jack.

"They are like us?" she asked timidly.

"Yep, just like us," I said, looking her right into her saucer sized eyes.

I looked at Lisa and added, "Mostly."

"Oh my god, she talks," exclaimed Jack. He quickly covered his mouth. He almost repeated the pool incident. This time he would have flown through the portal back into Mrs. Tenderschott's classroom instead of across the pool. Though I wasn't sure if Master Thomas' little booster he gave me was still working.

"Yes, she talks. Why exactly wouldn't she?" I asked. I think Jack realized how close he was to taking another flight, and held up his hands in defense.

"She's just so young," answered Lisa. She stood up, but still hadn't stopped smiling at Samantha. "I mean, she is what? A month old?"

"One month and four days."

"Accelerated," stated captain obvious.

"Yes, it would appear so," I responded to Jack. "Our best guess is she is five or six, and…" I ran across our room to my desk. The one I rarely used for homework. I threw open the same notebook that had been sitting there since I first arrived and tore out a piece of paper. I held that up away from me. "Watch this." I gestured towards Jack and Lisa, then towards Samantha. "Sam, knock this piece of paper out of mommy's hand, like you did the branch outside."

"You guys are allowed outside?" Jack asked, and I shushed him.

"Sam, go ahead. Knock this piece of paper out of my hand like you did outside with Master Thomas, Marie, and Jen."

Samantha held out both hands and at first, the paper waved back and forth. Then I felt the force push hard against it and it slipped out of my fingers.

"Holy crap!" exclaimed Jack.

"Hey, now. Language in front of my daughter, please." I scolded him.

"Sorry."

"Seriously Larissa. What Jack said. She can already do magic?" asked Lisa. Now it was her time to be wide eyed.

I nodded. "We," I looked at Mrs. Tenderschott because she was a part of this, "tested her two weeks ago and she is telekinetic. Just like me. That is all we know at the moment. We haven't tested anything else."

"Speaking of, grab your adorable little daughter and step on in. I have something that might help you with your magic." Mrs. Tenderschott disappeared through the portal and back into her room. Jack and Lisa followed her, keeping their eyes on us.

I grabbed Samantha by the hand and walked up to the portal. I looked at it, and the room on the other side. The next step I needed to take came with an uneasy feeling. So much so, I stopped and put my foot back down on the floor in my room. Mrs. Saxon had been clear when she restricted me to my room and the library. Any place outside of that was completely forbidden, as was talking to anyone else at the coven besides those instructors assigned to my training. Letting anyone else know I was out of Mordin, and here at the coven, was an absolute no-no. Master Thomas had my house arrest extended to a spot outside, but that was it. Going into a classroom and being around Jack and Lisa broke two rules at the same time. Breaking these rules would be Mrs. Tenderschott's fault, but even knowing that didn't silence that voice in my head, which was yelling at me to stop. Why was I having such a hard time with this, when just weeks ago, I practically dismantled Mrs. Saxon's runes to leave the coven against her will with everyone watching? Maybe that was why. Not to mention everything else that had happened.

"Come on," urged Mrs. Tenderschott.

"Does Mrs. Saxon know?" I asked, still unsure, and feeling like a prude.

"Well," thought Mrs. Tenderschott as she walked toward the spinning portal. She had a mischievous twinkle in her eye that I hadn't seen before. "She told me to fix you a potion. She didn't tell me I had to bring it up to you."

"And them?" I asked, remembering the stern warning about how dangerous it would be if something slipped and others found out I was here.

"Think about it like a jailbreak," Lisa said from behind Mrs. Tenderschott.

"Yep, that is what it is. A jailbreak. Rebecca isolated them to rooms away from the others, with access to a classroom or two for their studies. This is one of the classrooms, and I don't see any harm in letting the jail birds cross," reasoned Mrs. Tenderschott with a warm smile.

"Oh, but there is," I said, worriedly, as I stepped through the portal with Samantha. The aroma from her inventory of ingredients flooded our senses. It sent me down memory lane remembering the first time I walked in to here, but that trip was short-lived. As we walked further into the room, up to the front, another equally powerful stench overpowered them. It had to be a lesson gone bad. "The council is here... or at least Mrs. Wintercrest is here. She can't know I am here." I looked at Jack and Lisa and fretted. "You can't tell a soul you saw me or Samantha here. Promise?"

Lisa rushed over and hugged me. "We won't. Will you stop worrying? We kind of already knew." Lisa smirked at me.

"Master Thomas is conducting one of our classes in secret," added Jack.

"Well, that fink. He stressed many times how important it was to keep this all a secret."

"Larissa, relax," Mrs. Tenderschott said, as she pushed Lisa out of the way and hugged me. "No one is going to find out, and no one is going to see you here. The doors... are well... locked." She spun me around to face the back wall of her classroom where the doors should be, but there were no doors. As soon as I saw them, I giggled, and she spun me back around. "Now, just stop it. Where is that brazen young woman I knew that would break any rule placed in front of her?"

"That girl is gone. The price of breaking rules has cost her too much." My eyes looked away and avoided hers.

"Nonsense." Mrs. Tenderschott bent down and hugged Samantha. "Now give your auntie a big hug." Samantha didn't hesitate. She never did around her. She took to Mrs. Tenderschott like I did when I first met her. The woman had a disarming warmth. "I have something for you, too. It's up at the table."

I looked up at the front of the classroom at the infamous table that was the source of many a torture session when we were all trying to figure out just who and what I was. There, sitting in front of two stools, were two glasses. One was taller than the other, but there were two of them.

"Wait. I'm the one that needs the potion. Sam doesn't."

"Don't be silly," Mrs. Tenderschott said as she took her place on the other side of the table.

When I finally reached the stools, I knew what she meant about being silly. Mine was a potion. A vile smelling thing that looked worse than it smelled, if that was possible. Chunky red and brown. Like the leftovers from a horror film set.

The smaller glass had a sweet brown liquid in it topped with whipped crème. I lifted Samantha up on her stool, and she wasted no time running a finger through the whipped crème. She was born with a sweet tooth for food. I was the same way when I was younger, and somehow I recently rediscovered that. From time to time, I even stole a bite or two of ice cream from her bowl. I was still shocked it stayed down every time. Something had changed about me in that regard. I still didn't need to feed the traditional away, and hadn't developed the nerve yet to attempt a full meal of regular food. I doubted I ever would. Mrs. Saxon had worked out how to handle my needs in isolation better than I believed that cage in Mordin would have. One lukewarm glass of blood every three days. It worked, but wasn't as satisfying as the hunt and the kill, but it still provided what I needed. Theodora's private stash was hot and fresh, which made me a little envious of that life. This was like expecting filet mignon and getting ground chuck. It was still blood, but it didn't taste or feel the same going down. Marie was the lucky one. Jen and Kevin took her out on hunts. She was at least able to feel normal. I looked down at Samantha and remembered an earlier conversation. I had never let her see me feed, but I wondered. Should I test her next time to see if she can stomach a little sip? I shook that thought out of my head. If I was wrong, that would be a terrible experience for her, and who knew what she would think of her mother feeding on blood? We will keep it to hamburgers, ice cream, and the required vegetables for now, until she shows other vampire traits first.

"Go ahead, drink your hot chocolate," I said, giving her the permission she sat there and patiently waited for.

"Wait, she needs this... and this." Mrs. Tenderschott plopped a huge marshmallow in the middle of the mountain of whipped crème. Then she put a straw in the glass to make consuming the sugar rush easier. I was sure I was going to pay for this later.

An uneasiness overcame me when Lisa and Jack leaned over the table toward me. Both had their own cups in front of them. They were getting to enjoy the same treat Samantha was, but yet they kept glancing down at my glass, and then back at me. "What?"

Jack pointed down at my glass and asked, "You can't smell that?"

Oh, I could. I picked up a hint of it when I entered the room, and it got stronger the closer I got to it. Now, sitting there with it practically under my nose was torturous, but I did my best to act like I smelled nothing. Just once I wished a potion for me tasted good. "Smell what?" I said as I pushed it across the table.

"Nope. You have to drink it." Mrs. Tenderschott met me halfway, pushing the glass back to my side.

I looked down at Samantha and asked, "Want to trade?"

She gave me an emphatic shake of the head and took another long sip through her straw. I looked down at my glass, resigned to my fate.

"Can't you make a potion that tastes good?" I knew it was a fruitless question. Very few of the ingredients in the room smelled or tasted good, and combining them together just made them all worse. It was probably similar to that old saying, two wrongs don't make a right. In this instance, two piles of crap combined just make a bigger smellier pile of crap.

Mrs. Tenderschott replied by leaning over and pushing it closer to me.

I picked up the glass and held it up at eye level, trying to look through it. I couldn't see through the sludge. "Do I want to know what is in it?"

"Not before you drink it. Now go ahead."

Based on experiences, and what I knew about potions, that was probably for the best. I took another tentative look at my fate and then downed it. There was no point in just taking a sip. Knowing what it tasted like wouldn't make it any easier to drink. My iron clad stomach seemed more sensitive than normal. I blamed the human food I had been eating lately. It lurched at the intrusion. I held back my stomach's repulsive response and even faked a smile toward Jack and Lisa.

"So how long will it last?" I asked. That was a question I probably should have asked first.

"Not sure. I am not really sure it will work," replied Mrs. Tenderschott with a shrug of her shoulders.

"What? You don't even know if this will work?" I felt like a lab rat.

"Well," she started, and then looked at me, unsure. "You have always been a mystery. The combination of what you are always makes potions difficult. We never know if something will work until we try it. Why don't you try something?"

I stood up from the stool and backed away from the table. How to test it? I had countless options I could go with, but I felt I needed to start simple. That didn't mean I couldn't have a little fun with it. Focusing on the glass and the sludge that clung to its sides, I levitated it above the table, but I didn't stop there. The glass rose higher and drifted across the table, hovering over Jack and Lisa. That was where I used a little jerk of my hand to tilt it. A drop of the sludge slid toward the rim of the glass. Both scattered, knocking their stools over, and I returned the glass back to the table without spilling a drop.

Well, it worked, or it kind of did. After the glass settled on the table, I did a little test and wasn't too surprised to find everything still tangled up in chaos. Master Thomas appeared to be correct about this. Being right was a bad habit of his. His booster, and this potion, opened up some of my magic, but not all of it. That made me wonder about its limits. With a quick flick of my wrist, I produced a flame. It danced on the palm of my hand for a few moments before I let it turn into a ball that changed from bright red to blue. There was one more little trick I wanted to try, but not here. There was only one question that remained. "How long will it last?"

Mrs. Tenderschott shrugged. "Again, you are a mystery to us. In most witches, this could last a couple of hours, but don't fret." She walked over to a shelf to her left and retrieved a tray of glass jars that had a depressing familiar looking sludge in them. "I made extra so you can take it with you and drink it when you feel you need it. At least until you can do all this on your own."

"Larissa, do they know what has you all clogged?" asked Lisa.

"What doesn't have me clogged up?" I put air quotes around the phrase clogged up. It was really the best term to describe what was happening, and that was the best answer. It would seem everything does.

"But I don't understand," Lisa said, clearly confused as she walked back up to the table and sat on her stool.

"I don't either," added Jack. "You had it so together magically in New Orleans."

"Was it Mordin?" Lisa whispered, seemingly afraid to even say the name.

While that place definitely impacted me, it wasn't that. I knew what it was. Edward knew what it was, but I was sure it wasn't common news Mrs. Saxon shared around with everyone. Jack and Lisa didn't know I went back to find Nathan.

"I think that was it. Probably just the lingering effect of that place."

It was a flimsy reason, and I knew it, and by the way Lisa stared at me from the other side of the table, she knew it too. I needed to come up with something else to avoid digging a hole I couldn't get out.

"Larissa, what aren't you telling us?" Lisa leaned a little further over the table, pushing her point.

"Not a thing. I think you are right. It was Mordin. It was a dreadful place." My excuse crumbled right before my eyes. That didn't stop me from trying to add more details to prop it up enough for them to buy it and move on. "Dark, isolated, cold, and they block magic…"

"You can stop right there," Lisa interrupted me, and I saw the rest of it crumble to the floor. She wasn't going to buy this, no matter how much I tried to sell it. The thought of testing this potion again and using consumption on Lisa crossed my mind, but I thought better of it. That would only be temporary, and I couldn't bring myself to do it to a friend. Oh my God. Had I developed scruples?

"Chaos and disorder surround you. It's all a big mess right around here." Lisa waved her hands all around me.

"How can you tell?" Jack asked, looking at Lisa. Questions dripped from his eyes as he looked at me again. He practically stared a hole right through me with his intensity.

"It's something you can't see yet," explained Lisa.

"Why not?"

Lisa looked at me for help, but I let my eyes politely decline. She was on her own here. She said it, knowing that was a topic we needed to tread gently around, and it took the heat off me for a minute.

"You're not old enough?" she squeaked, scrunching up her face.

"You mean until I ascend?" Jack groaned.

Lisa just nodded, and Jack sank onto his stool.

"You only have two months," Lisa reminded him, but that didn't seem to improve his mood much. When she realized she couldn't console him anymore, she turned her attention back to me, much to my disappointment. I had hoped she had forgotten all about me. "Please tell me you and Nathan aren't fighting again. Larissa, he's a guy. He is going to do stupid stuff."

Lisa continued her rant, but I didn't hear any of it. My mind had checked out, and I looked at Mrs. Tenderschott. My eyes beseeched her for help. I could only hope she wouldn't decline my appeal like I had declined Lisa's just a few moments ago. From all appearances, she hadn't. There was a quick shake of her head at the question that we were both pondering, or had to be pondering. Could we tell them? That was an absolute no. We were bending Mrs. Saxon's rules enough already. That would shatter one. No one. Absolutely no one was to know what was really going on. Not with Mrs. Wintercrest and several members of the council here. There was too much to risk. Even Lisa and Jack knowing I was here was a huge risk that still made me uneasy.

"What?" Lisa abruptly asked. I think she finally realized we weren't paying any attention to her. "What happened?" Then, just as quickly as she had asked that question, Lisa seemed to find the answer on her own. Her eyes exploded open, wider than I had ever seen. Her brown eyes were lonely islands in a sea of white.

"Oh God!" she exclaimed and pointed in my direction. Then she repeated it, "Oh God!" with a hint of a wail. Lisa sprung up off her stool and ran around the table, practically tackling me with a hug. "I don't understand, but we can fix this. We can fix all of this."

"Fix what?" Jack asked, confused.

Mrs. Tenderschott and I both struggled to pry Lisa off of me. The emotionally charged room even had Samantha leaving her half full hot chocolate behind to wrap her arms around me.

"Nathan's not here." Lisa said. Her voice muffled against my shoulder.

"What? I don't understand." Jack looked around for answers.

"You of all people should—" replied Lisa, but Jack still stood there looking as clueless as ever. I was sure he felt my anguish. An emotion he probably chalked to any of the many events he knew about that could have, and probably should have, caused it. If he had known, he probably would have asked. I wouldn't have told him the truth if he did. I was still in the mode of the least they knew the better.

I hoped Lisa didn't really understand everything either, but I had a sinking feeling that somehow she did. There was more to this than her just putting two and two together. To truly make the leap to the truth, she would have needed help. That was assuming she actually knew the truth. It was entirely possible she had assumed that something else happened to Nathan. Like he had died in the skirmish shortly after I was taken, and before Mrs. Saxon saved everyone. A logical leap, and one that even just the thought of came close to breaking me, not that I wasn't already broken. That would explain her reaction.

"Do you know where he is? We can go get him." Lisa said as she finally released me. Well, sort of. Her hands traced down my arms until they reached my hands. She gripped them and looked deep into my eyes. Hers were compassionate and caring. I knew she meant it. She truly meant she would help in any way possible. Mine, I feared, were like a deer caught in the headlights. So were Mrs. Tenderschott's. We both knew we needed to know what Lisa thought she knew.

"It's all right. He will show up soon." I looked over her shoulder again at Mrs. Tenderschott for help. The vacant stare she returned told me she was just as lost as I was.

"Larissa!" Lisa jerked my hands. "How can you say that? It's dangerous for him to be out there with all that is going on. What if the witches attack New Orleans again? The only way to protect him is to bring him here."

Mrs. Tenderschott grabbed Lisa and turned her around, gently. "Lisa, why do you think they are going to attack New Orleans again?" When she asked, she glanced at me.

"Oh... I don't know. They did before. Jack and I both saw it start just before Mrs. Saxon pulled us back here. They might again."

Mrs. Tenderschott and I let out a collective sigh of relief. I even let a little air pass my lips.

"You saw it?" I asked and pulled her away from the table at the front and to the first row of tables. I pulled out two chairs, and she sat without a suggestion.

"Yes."

"What happened?"

Lisa pulled within herself. I had seen her do this before. She was remembering back to that day by taking herself back to it. Something she could do by tapping into a little of the dark magic she possessed. Her head looked up at the ceiling, then she spoke.

"It was only a few hours, maybe two, after they took you to Mordin. Jack, Laura, Apryl, and I were helping the wounded witches. More witches showed up, and we thought they were here to help. We were stupid enough to have some false hope that the council was going to look past the fact that these were rogue witches and actually help them. They didn't help. They didn't even come to the camp. They headed off into the woods. We saw flashes of every color and heard thunderous impacts and screams. Oh God, the horrible screams. Jack and Mike ran into the woods to find Nathan, but several witches attacked Mike before they made it too far. Jack defended him, but the attack eventually forced both of them out. After the witches left, Jack and I went and searched for Nathan. We didn't find him. We didn't really find any vampires that were still alive. Beheaded bodies littered the ground. We were still searching when Mrs. Saxon arrived at the farmhouse to bring us back here." Lisa's eyes cleared as she looked back at me.

"Larissa, we really tried to find him. We did. When Mrs. Saxon arrived, we told her what had happened and about Nathan, but she wouldn't let us go search again. We begged and begged. She told us he was still alive, and she would send someone to find him."

"Divination," I said, and Lisa looked back at me curiously. "That was how she knew. It seems Mrs. Saxon is rather expert at it, and she did send someone to find him. Jen and Kevin asked around and discovered he was the new coven leader.

Lisa let out a sigh, and her body shuddered. "Good. I was afraid he was still missing, and she was just telling us that to make us come back with her." Then she smirked and leaned forward, tapping me on the knee. "I used it myself to see you weren't going to see him later tonight. That was how I knew he wasn't here."

"Dang, you're getting really good at it."

"Practice," responded Lisa, while she polished her knuckles against her black hoodie. "But seriously. Let's go get him if you know where he is.

"What are you waiting for?" asked Jack. "The Larissa I know would have already yanked his ass back here."

"Well," I paused and wondered if I was going to cause any issue with telling them what I was about to. They already knew about the attack, and that he was okay. They don't know about the ongoing war between the witches and vampires, which, from all I was hearing, was a one-sided affair. My glance wandered over to Mrs. Tenderschott for any warnings as I started just in case my judgement was flawed. "I tried, and he wouldn't come back."

"What?" Lisa screamed, startling Samantha.

I picked her up and put her on my lap. It comforted her, but it comforted me more so. Lisa reached over and gave Samantha an apologetic rub on the arm. "We tried. Right after I gave birth to Samantha, Jen, Master Thomas, and I went back to New Orleans and found him in the mansion Jean ran the coven from. I tried to convince him to come home, but the attack by the witches, the one you saw, turned him against all of us. He doesn't trust any witches, even his mother, and he flatly refused to come back with us. Then he made us leave."

"You're kidding, right?" asked Jack.

I hugged Samantha a little tighter. "Nope. I wish I was, but I'm not."

Lisa pointed at me, and then stated, "That explains the chaos that surrounds you. That has to be it."

I nodded and then ducked my head. "That's what I think too, but I don't know what to do about it."

My head was still dipped down, with my chin buried on the top of Samantha's head. I gently kissed it. When I looked up, both Jack and Lisa were looking at Mrs. Tenderschott. "I'm sorry. There may be potions for matters of the heart, but there is nothing for this. She has no choice but to handle this the hard way.

"That's me, the hard way," I remarked.

"So, what now?" asked Lisa.

"Well, we wait." I didn't expand on what we were waiting for. Nathan? My magic? Some other miracle?

"Do you think he'll come back by himself?"

"I don't know." I didn't. It was one of a million things I didn't know. "I can only hope, but I don't know." I stood up off the stool, carrying Samantha. Her hot chocolate induced sugar rush had worn off, and she had become extremely comfortable and sleepy in my lap. "What I do know is I have an exhausted little girl here who needs a nap?"

Samantha offered a mild protest, but her own yawn ended it. Lisa walked over and gave me a hug. Jack acted like he wanted to do the same, but left it with a rub on the shoulder. "I'm sure Nate will come around. He has always been stubborn, but smart."

"I hope so." Hope was something I used to rely on, but lately it seemed so far from something real, I had lost my belief in it. Things that were concrete were where I focused. "I need to get this little girl back upstairs. Mrs. Tenderschott, could you?"

"Of course." She twirled open a portal into our room, and I stepped through it without hesitation. "Don't forget your goodies." Mrs. Tenderschott stepped through and placed the tray of glass jars containing all she had made of my little focus booster on the top of my dresser. I didn't want to forget those, but almost had. They were important to something I wanted to try later.

4

Oh, how I was jealous of my sweet little angel. She slept so soundly every night. It would be heavenly to close my eyes and drift away like she did, even if only for a few moments. Nights were the worst for me. Before, I had the activities on the roof to distract me. Even in New Orleans, my mind was constantly occupied. Even if some of that was self-inflicted dram, and lord knows, I was guilty of that from time to time. Now, there was nothing. Just me, holding Samantha as close as I could while she slept, and my nightly war against the thoughts that threatened to destroy my solitude. It was a battle I lost most nights. I even tried flicking through channel after channel of television shows with the volume down to avoid waking her. Nothing really helped. The thoughts always came. The hole where Nathan should have been always opened up, pulling me closer to the edge of a bottomless pit. My soul ached.

That was the most fitting description. It ached. I used to wonder if I even had a soul, being what I was and all, but losing Nathan like this answered that question loud and clear. I had one, and it was a large part of who I was, and every ounce of it was in pain. It screamed out for Nathan, and he wasn't there to answer. One night, I wondered if it might have been easier if he was truly gone. In some ways, it might. I would still miss him badly, but it would be easier to accept. Instead, he was out there choosing not to be with me. He was choosing to not be with me for a stupid reason that he was wrong about. Making matters worse, there were others manipulating him. They wouldn't let him open his eyes enough to see past all the lies. I knew in my heart if he did, he would come home, but I also didn't see that happening. Everything that had, and was, happening out there just fueled his anger and confusion. Like gas on a campfire. He was probably now a full on forest fire raging out of control.

I no longer wept with the ache. For a while, I thought I ran out of tears, but occasionally Samantha did something that would bring a tear or two of joy surging forward. I now believed the pain I felt was too deep for tears. That it was so deep that it suppressed the activity of crying, along with everything else, including my magic. All I could do was sit there, staring off into nothingness, letting the world whirl around me. That was me, a stone in a creek with the rapids of life crashing around me, wearing down my edges. That was even me when I held Samantha all night long. While I sat there, thoughts after thoughts flooded my mind. All about

Nathan. All missing him. All tearing chunks at the edges of the hole I felt in my soul, making it larger and pulling me further into it. I needed him. I needed him with every fiber of my being, and so did Samantha. That always tore at me badly, but it wasn't the worst of all. What really tore large gapping chunks from the edge of the hole was how badly Nathan needed us. He really needed us. So much of his life had changed, and he needed us to help him adjust. He needed his family to show him the way, to show him why he was important, to show him we love him. To know we weren't there for him hurt me worst of all.

That was why I was sitting here pondering something that I knew was wrong. Well, wrong was relative. What I was considering was strictly forbidden, and it may be a moot point. I wasn't even sure it was possible. That didn't stop me from trying. I stood up and walked to the center of the room, still arguing with myself about what I was about to do. The argument wasn't about whether I should do this from a perspective of right or wrong. I had already rationalized that part of it, like I always did. I had concerns about being able to pull it off. That was why I leaned back and peeked with one eye when I spun my arm around and thought of the cove. There was a little spark and the hint of an opening, but I stopped before it fully formed. That was enough to answer my question. Mrs. Tenderschott's horrible tasting potion gave me enough juice to open a portal.

I looked at Samantha and knew this was for her. That was what I told myself, even though I knew full well this was also for me. Using some of my restored ability, I witch-whispered through the wall to Marie. "Can you come over?"

She entered my door in seconds. She and Jen were the only people Mrs. Saxon had excluded from her spell that locked my door. Everyone else that knew I was here was a witch, and could just use a portal.

She hugged me instantly, and I asked, "Can you watch her for a few minutes? Just in case she wakes up."

"Yes. Yes, of course," she answered, confused. Which I knew she would be.

"And don't tell a soul what you are about to see."

Now that request received a look even more confused than the first.

I held my hand out and thought about the mansion in New Orleans on Audubon, but stopped before my arm moved. One of the many nagging questions about my current state had taken over my mind, and I was glad it did. I might have done something completely foolish. Not that it would be the first time I had. I just needed to be careful. The stakes were way too high.

To solve my nagging problem, I went over and uncapped one of the jars Mrs. Tenderschott had prepared. The smell hit the room, and my stomach lurched. Marie covered her nose. Samantha was sound asleep, but even she turned away from it. I was sure she smelled something rotten in whatever dream she was having. To save them from any more stink, I picked it up and gulped it all.

Marie gagged. "How can you drink that?"

"It's not the worst thing I have had to drink around here," I whispered back, remembering all the other portions they had subjected me to since I arrived at the coven. And what was Marie complaining about? She had me drink water when that usually would have caused severe vomiting.

Now I felt I was ready and took my spot in the room and spun my arm around. A portal opened to the room with the large wooden throne.

"Wait! What?" Marie grabbed my arm. We both looked back to make sure Samantha hadn't woken up. She was still sound asleep.

My hand met Marie's on my arm. "I need to go look. I have to, and now that I sort of have my magic back, I can." Or I hoped I could. I didn't know how long this lasted. Nor had I tested out everything. "Um... I'm going to leave this open just in case. Don't let anyone come through it."

"Who would come through it?" Marie asked as I stepped through.

"Don't know."

That same smell of old blood hit me just like it had before. This time felt different, though. Before you felt someone was there, and the place looked lived in. Now it was desolate, and whoever had been here left in a hurry. Pieces of furniture were strewn around, and the grand glass doors that lead to the ballroom were shattered. Even the doors that lead from the ballroom out to the outside courtyard were just empty wooden frames. The wind whipped in through the openings.

I continued down the hall and past the dining room. If anyone other than Jean had ever lived in this place, I was sure there were many grand family meals around the large dark wood table that sat in the middle of the room. Probably a few Thanksgiving feasts with turkey, dressing, and all the trimmings. Feast in our world was slightly different, and I saw evidence that one had taken place here. The smell was rancid and old, but I still knew what it was. When I passed two full goblets of blood sitting on the table, I knew no one else was here. I grabbed one goblet; it was cold to the touch. I tried to swirl the contents around, but it had mostly congealed into some mixture of solid and liquid. It had been here for days, and its source was probably the rancid smell that wafted in from the kitchen on the breeze.

I went in the kitchen to check it out. Why? Who knows? Maybe on the off chance that Nathan was in there feasting on whatever was rotting. Let me take that back. Whatever had already rotted. A single deer, or what remained of a deer, lay on the floor with the stains of its own blood pooled around it. Maggots feasted on what remained of its flesh. I sat there and watched them for a while. Their movements were hypnotic. Chaotic order. The mass moved around with a purpose. Maybe that was why they caught my attention. The order. The way the universe used to look to me. Now it was anything but. And there in that horrible smelling place, I found an example of what I was missing. That was probably why I didn't see him off in the corner, feasting on a rat that came for some of the deer's entrails. I didn't see him, but I heard him.

"You!" he screeched, as he stumbled out of the darkness. The rat dangled from his grasp. A finger on his other hand pointed at me as he screamed again, "You!"

When he crossed over into the moonlight and tripped over the deer carcass, I saw who it was and wanted to scream it back at him. It was him. Mr. Top Hat from my last visit. We didn't exactly leave on good terms, and we still weren't. I retreated from the kitchen to create some distance. But he kept coming, stumbling, and wobbling like a drunk, but he wasn't. He was weak and injured.

"You have the nerve to come back here?" he asked, falling from the door frame to the table. He knocked both goblets of stale blood to the floor. He paid no attention to the puddle of blood on the floor or the loud clang they made on impact.

"I'm looking for Nathan Saxon. Where is he?" I asked while I gave up more ground, backing into the hallway.

Mr. Top Hat just chuckled at my question.

"Please, tell me where he is."

Now out in the hall, he braced himself against the wall and lunged toward me. I stepped back, and he fell flat on the floor at my feet, and coughed, "No."

His bony hand reached out and tried to grab my ankle as I stepped back again. It shook and then fell to the floor, along with his head.

"Tell me where he is," I demanded again.

He pushed up off the floor and made it up to one knee. With labored movements, he lifted his head and threw it back proudly, and grinned widely at me. "Why? So, you can kill him? You made a mistake coming back here."

I was about to explain that I wasn't there to hurt or cause Nathan any harm, and I wasn't like the other witches. Not that I felt I could convince him I was the solution, but maybe I could convince him I wasn't part of the problem. He was probably there when I was taken prisoner by my own kind. I could have reminded him of that to help, but I never had the chance. Before I could even utter one word, he yelled, "Witch!"

The building came alive with movement. Vampires rushed in through the broken doors and windows. Maybe half a dozen or more. I didn't stand still long enough to count them. The time for talking had passed. I hoped they were as weakened as Mr. Top Hat, but if they were, they didn't show it. They were fast on my heels, and I was moving as fast as I could in those first five steps. A hand scratched down my back and I spun around. My instincts took over, and thank God Mrs. Tenderschott's potion didn't fail me. Two large orange balls of fire left my hands, hitting and sending their targets back against the wall.

In the impact's flash I saw five vampires, counting Mr. Top Hat, standing ready to fight. I felt a sickening wave come over me. Is this all that's left of the New

Orleans coven? Please God no. I needed to know. "It doesn't have to be this way. Just tell me where Nathan Saxon is."

"It won't be that easy. Your kind has to pay." Mr. Top Hat declared with a finger pointed right at me. All five crept closer, ignoring the two balls of fire I had in my hands, ready to launch.

I stepped back each time they stepped forward. We had already passed the ballroom and were now entering the room with the wooden throne. The spinning portal I left cast everything in a golden glow. Marie watched through the opening and acted like she wanted to step through, but I shook my head.

"Look," I decided to try some diplomacy. "I know what the witches did." I needed to talk fast. We were no longer in the hall, and the angry horde had fanned out around me. "And they were so wrong. I promise you, in the end, we will hold them responsible, but–"

So much for diplomacy. Two vampires lunged at me from the left, and as I turned to fend them off, sending them flying against the wall, the two to my right took their shot. I still had the balls of fire in my hands and backhanded them in their direction. Mr. Top Hat rushed me from the front and actually got a hand on me before my telekinesis sent him flying up to the ceiling. On his way down, I gave him a more traditional punch to remind him I was also a vampire, and just as strong as he was. He landed on the floor with a thud. Another hand grabbed my shoulder, and I pushed it away just in time for two more to grab me. I looked back at the portal and Marie had stepped one foot through. She knew it at the same time I felt it. I was losing this fight. I went limp and fell to the floor, slipping through their grasp. Then I threw myself toward the portal, while sending a few fireballs in their direction. That slowed them down, but didn't stop them. Hatred, which was a powerful emotion, fueled them.

With a strong wind, I shoved Marie Norton back through the portal. I followed quickly behind her, but not before sending another fireball back toward the vampires. I didn't realize how close one of them was. He reached for me but missed. When I fell to my floor, I spun my arm to close the portal, and it snapped shut. His severed arm fell to the floor, and Marie shrieked, waking up Samantha. I used a quick sleeping spell, and whispered, "sonno." She fell back asleep, and I felt like the worst parent in the world. I just used magic on my child, but that felt like a better option than letting her see the severed limb flopping around on the floor. I opened a small portal to the middle of the Mississippi River and let it jerk and jump its way out before I closed it.

"Well, that didn't work how I expected." Well, not entirely. Something felt better, though. At least for a second during the heat of the fight, I felt in control. More than I had when I drank the potion earlier. Maybe it was just the adrenaline talking.

5

"What did you expect to find?" Marie asked, almost scolding me.

"Nathan." That was the obvious answer, which Marie had probably already guessed in her head.

"I could have told you he wasn't there," she answered, and then grabbed me by the hands and pulled me over to the chair. I sat without being told to. This felt almost natural, and why wouldn't it? She had done this many times over the last seventy years when we needed to have a serious talk about something.

"Jen and Kevin heard weeks ago that what remained of the New Orleans coven had splintered and left the area. Only a few stragglers remained. They checked around, and other than a few that showed up at other covens where they had family members or friends, they didn't know where they went."

Hopelessness dragged my head down, but ever the positive one, Marie reached under my chin and propped it back up. Her black eyes mastered what I couldn't. She could show emotions, deep, powerful emotions. I lost count of how many times I tried the replicate her looks in the mirror, but each time I saw the same expressionless eyes staring back at me. She told me once that how she did it was her little secret. Whatever the secret, it worked every time, and I felt her compassion wrap me in a warm blanket.

"Larissa, relax. Nathan is still alive. You saw him when you went back there, and since then, the Jen and Kevin have heard mention of him. They just don't know where he is. It's only a matter of time before he shows up, and you and her," she turned around to look at Samantha, "can be the family you all need to be." Her hand brushed up my cheek and then ran through my hair as she stood up in front of me. "In the meantime, take it easy and try not to mess things up here. Mrs. Saxon was awfully nice to take you back in. Don't betray her trust by breaking her rules. What you did tonight was stupid. What would happen if you got caught?"

I doubted it would surprise Mrs. Saxon at this point. There wasn't really a rule left of hers I hadn't broken, but there was something about confessing that to Marie that I just couldn't make myself do.

"I know. It was stupid," I conceded to avoid a lecture. Maybe it was, but I had to try, and if I had any new information about where to look, I would try again. Where could I find any new information? Now, that was the question.

"Good," Marie said. "Now, are you going to try anything else stupid tonight?"

I shook my head while I looked past her at the stack of books still on the floor next to my bed. The same ones Edward had sent up months ago with that huge warning. That warning still played in my head, but it was a little softer than before. Probably because I had made a few trips already, but those were just trips out of my body. Controlling where I was going was another question. I think I sort of understood how to move around, or at least I had the basics of it. But the biggest question was buried in books one and three of that stack. That was how to find someone and then how to get to them. Nothing we had discussed so far with Mary Smith came close to covering that. It would seem I have some reading ahead of me tonight.

"So, how do we get another chair?" Marie looked around. If she had understood how this place worked, she would have been more specific with her request. A single wooden chair appeared right next to her as soon as she finished the question. "Oh, wow!"

"You get used to it." I remembered my first few days here. I wasn't surprised when the chair arrived, but her request surprised me.

"It's not what I had in mind, though, but I guess it will do." Marie inspected the chair and then pulled it to the center of the room.

"Well, what did you want?"

"Something comfortable enough to sit down and have a good old-fashioned movie night on while I keep you out of trouble," Marie said with a wink. My plans for a night of reading were no longer an option, and I knew better than to protest. Her little statement—to keep you out of trouble—told me she would view any protest I made as me trying to get her out of here so I could get into more trouble.

"Okay then." I thought of a small comfortable loveseat, and the chair turned into a comfortable cushioned seat for two with pillows. If we had more room, I would have gone for a whole pullout sofa so we can get comfy, but this would work. "Is that better?"

"Yep." She plopped down on it and patted the cushion next to her. I rolled my eyes and took a seat next to her. She leaned against its arm, and I leaned against her. This was a common arrangement for us. We had settled in, and I was getting comfortable, just as Marie sat up a little and looked around the room. "Where's the remote?"

Now, for a while, that would have been a good question. I never used it, but lately I needed it, and I knew exactly where it was. It was on the nightstand next to the bed. I summoned it, but Marie snatched it in mid-air before I had a chance to catch it. Not that there was any question who was going to be in charge of picking what we watched.

Throughout the night, we watched five movies, all from the 1930s and 40s. I don't know why, but it's comforting to watch one of those movies. When Samantha woke, she was surprised and happy to see Marie there. To her, she was like a grandmother. I guess she was, kind of. She had been a mother to me. At some point, when I had better control of my magic, I needed to introduce her to my actual mother.

After a rather silly breakfast, Marie offered to entertain Samantha while I did what I told her was studying for my magic training. I told her I had a ton of reading to do for my next lessons with Master Thomas and Mrs. Saxon. It was related in a way. It just probably wasn't something we would cover for quite a while. Our focus was the basics, and this reading was anything but basic.

At my desk, with the giggle crew behind me, and some talking pig on the TV, I cracked open the first of the seven books in the stack. This was the second time I had cracked it open. The first time was just to skim through it. The content and the warning fascinated me. Then it was my path to find Marie. Now it was my path to find Nathan, and I was doing more than skimming the pages. I couldn't have done much more before. I didn't understand enough yet. Now I knew more. Did I know enough? That was the question.

My first two hours of reading told me one thing. There were dozens of ways to find someone, but each had its own challenges. It was easy to find a blood relative. There were simple spells you could use to find out if they were alive, and even where they were. That had me thinking. If you knew where they were, would you really need astral projection to go to them? Couldn't you just use a portal to go see them? Heck, just get a train ticket. That might be a simpler approach, but as with everything, there was a challenge. If you weren't familiar with the area and couldn't visualize it, you couldn't open a portal to it. My train ticket idea sounded better all the time.

For those that weren't blood relatives, which would include Nathan, it was slightly more complicated. Which is exactly what Edward told me before. You could use a memory of the person and track their aura, but that was extremely difficult, and even the book contained several paragraphs of warnings. It was everything from some have similar auras to issues with nailing down the time and place of the memory.

The method I read that held some hope was called, "Blood of my Blood". The name initially sounded more fitting for a vampire related spell, but after I read it, the name made sense. You had to combine biological material of the person you sought, or that of a direct blood relative, with a potion. The ingredient list of the potion wasn't that daunting. Even if it was, I wasn't about to let something like that stand in our way. This held too much promise for me to dismiss it. I had to imagine there was a hair or something in his room down in Mrs. Saxon's apartment. Then it hit me, and I felt stupid. I looked back at Samantha, who was coloring with Marie. We had a blood relative, and a source of his blood.

Now, if we ignored my current problems with magic and my complete lack of confidence with potions, then we had a solution. Or make that part of a solution. Getting back was a problem. It appeared you were all on your own and your astral projection skills. The last two books in the stack of seven covered that topic. I had to get through four books to reach those two. I wanted to skip ahead, but a little voice, Edward's, stopped me and brought me back to Earth. The weight of his warning pressed down on me firmly. Playing with the unknown seemed dangerous, not that I wasn't one to take risks or leap before I looked, but that was the old me. This was the new Larissa. One that was a little less impulsive than before. I had a lot more at stake now, and was going to have to do this by the book. That meant I had a lot of reading ahead of me, but that reading would have to wait until later this afternoon. I had a morning session with Master Thomas, then therapy with Edward. Oh, the joys of my daily schedule. What I wouldn't give to be back in classes again.

Resigned to have a day that felt just like the one before it and the ones before that, I walked over to the tray of jars and opened another booster to help me with the simple things. I still hadn't figured out how long the effects lasted. I drank one before my little adventure and then, for the rest of the night and morning, I didn't really have any troubles. The entire time I was reading, I never touched a page to turn it. I just did it using magic. It was my way of testing to see if I still had it. If I was going to have to rely on this, I needed to know its limits. Even after three glasses of this goop, I could honestly say the taste hadn't grown on me. If possible, it got worse the longer it sat there.

It wasn't more than a few moments before a portal opened in the room and Master Thomas walked in. He, nor Mrs. Saxon, bothered using the door, not wanting anyone to see them coming in and out. I was still the biggest secret in the coven, or make that one of the secrets. There were a few others besides me.

"It's a good thing I wasn't getting dressed," I remarked, half joking, but half not. There was a frustration building from my house arrest. It just added on to the frustration of not being able to control my magic. Both were freedoms I had taken for granted until they were taken away from me.

"I listened in and heard Samantha and Marie, so I figured it was safe." He said as his glance regarded Marie. I knew what the question was on his mind.

"I opened a portal for Marie. You can relax."

Marie said nothing. Thank God.

Master Thomas walked over to the tray and inspected the three empty jars. He was even brave enough to take a sniff from one. An act for which the putrid odor richly rewarded him. I had to give him credit; he held back the urge to vomit like a champ, holding his mouth shut through two lurches. At least he didn't have to drink it.

"So, these actually work?" He gagged his way through the question.

"Surprisingly, yes." I floated the book I had on the desk back to the stack next to my bed. Master Thomas appeared to be amazed.

"How powerful are the effects?" He put the last jar down and tightly screwed on its top.

"Well. I can do most of the basic stuff, but that is about it. The world is still chaos."

"Crap."

I heard it, but couldn't believe what I heard. Master Thomas just swore under his breath. I knew what he was hoping. It was the same thing as I was. If it cleaned up that side of the magical world for me, we could finally get into the training I really needed.

"Sorry," I said, feeling the need to apologize. It appeared I wasn't the only one growing frustrated with the current situation.

"Oh no," he quickly corrected me with a hand wave, and then pulled a handkerchief from the pocket in his red suede jacket. He dabbed along the edges of his mouth and then replaced it. "It's not your fault, and it's only temporary."

I kept expecting to hear him utter, "I hope", but he didn't. He straightened up his posture, almost like righting himself, and took a few steps from the tray of offending liquid. "We should take advantage of it, though. Magic is like a muscle. The more you use it, the stronger it is. Maybe this," he pointed with a thumb back over his shoulder at the tray, "can be a bridge to make you right as rain."

6

After a surprisingly uplifting morning session with Master Thomas, I survived another session on the couch with Dr. Edward. The magic session was uplifting in that I could actually do something. I was sure the potion of rot Mrs. Tenderschott had prepared for me was responsible. Nevertheless, it was something. I felt... normal.

My session with Edward went like the others, and big surprise, we had a breakthrough. The source of all my problems stemmed from the emotions I felt when Nathan rejected me. What an astute observation and take away from our many sessions. I had to wonder if Edward had read any Freud books since our last session. What I needed to know now was how to fix it? Other than the obvious, go find the boy, yank him back here, bring his heart back around to some sense of reality, stop the war, replace the supreme, and save the world from complete and utter chaos. That seemed simple enough.

I didn't tell him that I saw that as the only path to fixing my issues. I was still a little leery of my newfound trust with Mrs. Saxon, and yes, I absolutely believed Edward was reporting back to her. I knew he was. They discussed my issues openly in front of me. I had already suggested going to find Nathan and bringing him back more than once to Mrs. She warned sternly against that. It wasn't a–you can't leave the coven–warning. It was more of one of those very mature–patience will win the day–warnings. The problem was, I didn't have that kind of patience.

What I asked Edward for was help to compartmentalize, or better yet, isolate all this junk in my head so I could clear away some of the clutter and open things back up. I wasn't so naïve to think that I could go get Nathan in my current state. My last little side-trip reinforced that. Just like any good therapist, Edward turned around and asked me how I thought I could clear my mind. Thank God I wasn't actually paying him. At the end of our session, he gave me a few books. Spiritual text, he believed, might help center me. As soon as I saw the dust covered jackets, I kind of blocked out anything else he said about them. I already had some light reading that I felt was more important.

My afternoon session with Master Thomas was outside again. Another detail that made it up lifting. I had grown tired of my own four walls. Not that I couldn't change them or expand them anytime I wanted. It was the air inside that was becoming too familiar for my liking. Mrs. Saxon was out there too, but not to teach. She was there to spend time with Samantha while she cast disapproving looks in my direction each time I stumbled over something easy. Toward the end of this session, I found the expiration period of Mrs. Tenderschott's potion. It was about six hours. As it wore off, I kept trying little things. Some worked, and some didn't.

At the end of its effectiveness, I felt adventurous and when no one was looking; I attempted to throw a combination of symbols like I learned from my father's notes, just to see if I could with what little I had left. It had come easily for me down in New Orleans, but it wasn't like riding a bike. I needed to see the symbols and the fabric of the universe they rode on. I needed to see the shape of the lines it created as I conjured it, but now all I saw was a tangled mess. That didn't mean I didn't try. I went for the lunar spiral and the chalice. Neither of which I had tried before. Even just by themselves. I felt these were safe to try. The ones I knew well were all combat or defensive symbols. If something went wrong with one of those, who knew what would happen? These, I doubted anyone would even notice, and if they worked, maybe they would help. Both were related to different parts of a woman's connection with nature. I felt, or hoped, they would help strengthen what remained of that connection I used to have. But there was another part of it, too. Intuition was one of those natural abilities more associated with women. These were amplifiers of sort for it along with mindful subconscious connections and psychic abilities. Each seemed like it led to a clearer mind, and maybe, just maybe, those would offer me some clarity here. At least that was what I had hope. My father's journal had many entries around these and his usage of them. They were a way to clear his palette in between complex spells that had many steps. That was kind of what I needed, and I felt it was worth a chance. What did I have to lose?

My conjuring was rather embarrassing, and it proved I needed more practice at this, and possibly more of that pungent booster. The chalice is a cup. Basically, a drinking glass with a stem, and the lunar spiral looks like the side of a snail's shell. The best –dad please forgive me– I could do was replace the actual vessel on top of the stem with the spiral. Who knew if the quality of the combination impacted its effectiveness? Maybe it was like a potion. Miss the mixing instructions by just a bit, or maybe a stir too many, and poof, you have complete and utter crap. I had six more jars of crap up in my room.

I made room for the combination in my head and visualized it. I waited for it to draw itself repeatedly, faster on each pass, but all it did was hang there. I had almost given up when I remembered the advice Mrs. Saxon had given about Nathan. Patience. Why did that show up now? I didn't know. I checked over my shoulder to ensure she wasn't watching me or planting the suggestion as a caution. But she was off playing hide and seek with Samantha and Jen Bolden. When I focused back on the symbols, they hung there burning. A wave of excitement came over me, along with various questions. Was it possible that one of the symbols, or the combination, was what brought up the advice from Mrs. Saxon at just the right time? That was too corny and maybe I was reaching, but it was possible. Just like the calming effect I felt come over me. Was I relaxed because it seemed I did something, or was this the effect of what I did? Either way, I would take it. It wasn't the most powerful of spells, but it was something. I looked again at the fabric of the world, and it was still jumbled in front of me. There were a few offshoots from the rats-nest that tried to reach out and surround me in something that looked round. As it did, I thought about what it could mean. The shape was always representational of what it was. Attacks were sharp waves that radiated out. Defensive were surrounding shields. This was a cocoon of sorts, protecting me, but protecting me from what? The mess that was my life?

The thoughts and darkness that had consumed me for weeks moved aside and allowed a calming feeling to enter. I did it. That had to be it. It was small, but I still did it. The lines surrounded me tighter, but I didn't let that concern me. The calming feeling inside grew, and I even felt my body relax. A voice inside, one I didn't recognize, but one that was soothing to hear, told me the order of my life. It was Samantha, my magic, and then Nathan. Then, just as clearly as it told me the order, it told me not to worry about any of it. Nature had a way, and no matter what I did, I couldn't change it. Things will happen when they happen.

I heard it. I understood it, and even more important, I believed it. I completely believed it. Like a compass needle pointing the direction for me to follow. Even then I saw some strings of the mess in front of me untangle themselves and lay down, back where they should be. This was just a stupid random test of myself, but it had accomplished so much more than I had expected. With all the searching and asking of others, the answer was just this, but I didn't fret over not realizing it myself. I even laughed. No one else made this suggestion either. Of course, why would they? Only my father knew how to do this. That pride I felt before about all he had accomplished welled up inside. This was great, right until I heard a second voice, this one I clearly knew to be that belonging to Nathan Saxon. It was full of panic and pain, and it said two words: "Help me!"

The sound of his voice gave me life, but his tone and words took it away just as fast. It both lit an inferno inside me and froze me to my core, all at the same time. I collapsed into a dizzying spin. I don't remember hitting the ground. As far as I knew, I was still falling. In the distance, I heard Samantha cry a very weak, "Mom?" I couldn't respond from where I was. I couldn't even see her. It was all black.

7

The next sight I saw was the ceiling of my room. I was lying there on my bed. Something I never ever did. Samantha was sitting next to me, rubbing my forehead, and looking down at me. She looked concerned. Her eyes were red, and tears streamed down her face. One hung on her chin. I reached up and softly brushed it away. "Hey. I'm okay."

She fell down on the bed and hugged my neck. "You scared us."

"You scared all of us," repeated Mrs. Saxon, who watched from the corner of the room.

I sat up, still holding Samantha, who, if my imagination wasn't playing with me, had gotten taller. A lot taller. I had to swing her legs beside me as I sat up. No one else was in the room. Just Mrs. Saxon and Samantha, and that felt a little odd. I didn't know why. Who was I expecting to be there? I thought, and my mind still felt somewhat clear, but there was something there. Something I couldn't put my finger on. It wasn't a thought or a memory. Just something on my mind, as cliché as that sounded.

"Sorry, I don't know what happened."

"Not a problem," Mrs. Saxon said as she walked over to the bed. Samantha let go of the python grip she had around my neck and sat next to me. Then Mrs. Saxon sat on my other side. What a sweet family portrait this was. Three generations of Saxons. Well, maybe not. I wasn't officially one, since Nathan and I weren't married—yet. I was his baby momma. Which was a term Mrs. Saxon hated. I hadn't told Samantha who her father was yet. So, she had no clue Mrs. Saxon was her grandmother. That was something I wanted to wait to do until Nathan was here. Again my, probably stupid, desire for Samantha to learn about her father from her father. The only things ruining this perfect picture were the tears running down Samantha's cheeks and the look in Mrs. Saxon's eyes.

"What happened?" I turned and asked the only person in the room who likely knew or had a good chance of knowing.

Then I saw it. Another first. The first time Mrs. Saxon looked past me to my daughter, my much older looking daughter who looked about eight years-old now, and shared a knowing look with her. Now I knew it. Everyone knew what had happened, except me. As I looked at Samantha again, and brushed her long red hair over her ear, I wondered exactly how long I had been out.

"Well," started Mrs. Saxon, who fidgeted. "The better question is, what do you remember?"

What did I remember? Now that was a good question. Not a whole hell of a lot. Wait. That wasn't right. I remembered a few things. "We were outside doing training with Master Thomas, and you two," I pointed back and forth between Mrs. Saxon and Samantha. "You were playing hide and seek in the woods." And that was about it. Every time I tried to connect the dots between that moment and when I woke up here. It was like someone had erased a portion of my memory. "Then I woke up here."

"Nothing else?" asked Mrs. Saxon.

I shook my head while biting my lip. Why did I have a feeling that wasn't a good thing?

"What if I was to tell you, you had a magical overload and crossed into something you weren't ready for and passed out?"

"I'd say... it's not the strangest thing I've heard," I admitted reluctantly, and felt an uneasy inkling that this wasn't even the strangest part of this event. "With everything going on with my magic, I guess anything is possible." I shrugged. "A magical overload?"

"Yes, it can and does happen, but I didn't tell you the best part." Mrs. Saxon said with a smile, a proud smile at that. I felt Samantha squirm around to face me. "Samantha caught you. She saw you fall and caught you with magic and lowered you lightly down to the ground."

"You did?" I spun around. She sat there with a wide grin and then grabbed my hands.

"I did. I did it just like you and Master Thomas told me. I imagined a rope and wrapped it around you and pulled until you stopped."

"Oh my god," I hugged her. My little girl was growing up so fast, and becoming quite an accomplished little witch. Then I remembered where I last saw her standing, and let go of her. "Wait, you were off in the woods. You had to be a couple hundred feet away from where I was standing." I looked back and forth between the two of them, confused. To do something like that, that quick, over that distance was a truly remarkable feat. I wasn't even sure I could do something like that when everything was working right.

"She did, and yes, it was that far."

"Woooow," I said and turned back to Samantha. "Very nice." She was so proud; she could barely keep still. "Well, thanks for saving old mom out there. I can't promise it will be the last time. I have a history of doing stupid things." That got a laugh from Samantha, and behind me, I heard a little snicker, which annoyed me and caused me to turn back to Mrs. Saxon.

"So, speaking of doing stupid things, what exactly did I do? I'm fairly sure I don't want to do it again?"

"Well, that I'm not exactly sure." Mrs. Saxon patted me on the leg. "See, after Sam caught you, I placed a block on your memories to stop any further damage."

I had to shake my head and rub my eyes at that. "You put a block to stop damage. What kind of damage?"

Mrs. Saxon got up off the bed and walked over to Samantha with a hand extended. She accepted it. Then she spun her other arm around and opened a portal. "Samantha, I need to talk to your mother for a minute. Why don't you spend some time with Mrs. Tenderschott? I think she wants to show you your first potion."

I heard Mrs. Tenderschott laugh and call Samantha in through the portal. My girl, my growing girl, practically ran through the portal, which closed as quickly as Mrs. Saxon had opened it.

"Is it me, or is she almost a foot taller than just a few days ago?" I asked, almost amazed at what I had just seen. Just last month, I held her in my arms for the first time. She took her first steps a few days after that. Her first words came later that same day.

"So, it isn't just me?" Mrs. Saxon asked, still staring at the space where the portal had been. "And her control of magic is advancing fast. She is easily where someone should be at age ten."

"She is my little girl," I remarked, trying to be cute and humorous, but it fell flat. Mrs. Saxon's face turned serious as she looked back.

"I asked her to go someplace else because the only way to find out what you did to put yourself in that state is to unblock your memories of that moment."

"Which... I'm guessing is slightly dangerous?" Trying to make the leap across the enormous cavern left in Mrs. Saxon's explanation.

"More than slightly dangerous. It puts you right back where you were just before your brain shut down," she explained.

Okay, so that sounded more than just slightly dangerous. I did something that overloaded me and put me out, and the only way to find out what I did was to return to the moment it happened. That would be a big no, or make that it should have been a big no. Except, I needed to know what it was, so I wouldn't do it again. I hopped up off the bed and started pacing while biting on my thumbnail, something I hadn't done since, well, long before I became a vampire. My mother used to jump me for the nasty habit, but it was something I did when I was nervous, and yep, I was extremely nervous at the prospects of what we were discussing.

"Larissa, you don't really have anything to worry about. I will be right there with you and will stop things before it becomes too much for you."

Well, that sounded simple enough, but it didn't keep my mind from racing through all sorts of crazy events and outcomes. "What if you can't stop it before it overloads me again?" I asked, as if I knew how this worked.

Mrs. Saxon stood there as confident as ever. Her posture was straighter than any vampire I knew. With her arms crossed and without a hesitation, she replied, "I can, and I will. Trust me."

My mouth opened, ready to mouth my agreement, but second thoughts kept speeding in. It was those that fueled what finally came out of my mouth. 'What if I get overloaded right from the beginning and it can't be stopped because it happens immediately upon starting? What about that?'

"Come now," she looked down her nose at me. "You don't think I would have put the block so close to the event, do you? I'm a smarter witch than that." She approached me, hand extended, just like she had Samantha a few moments earlier, and then led me back to the bed. I was still making a meal out of the thumbnail on my other hand when I sat.

"Try to relax," she suggested, and then smirked at herself. "I know. You are tired of hearing that. I'm going to enter your memories. You won't feel anything." She placed both of her hands against my temples. "Let's take a walk through your memories," she whispered and closed her eyes.

"Wait! This is going to work, right? I mean, you said you see events before they happen all the time, so you know this is going to work out, right?" It was a fair question. The woman had told me before she knew all the trouble I was going to cause, and she already knew how things would end.

"This isn't a big enough event on the road for me to even see, so it's nothing to worry about."

"The road analogy again? I get it."

Her eyes were still closed, but she smiled pleasantly. "I see someone taught you well. This isn't even a pebble on that road, so that should tell you something. Now let's start."

Her hands pressed lightly against my temples. "Wait. I have one more question. Why didn't you see it at least coming?"

"Not even a spec of sand on the road of your life. Now, stop delaying us. Close your eyes and follow me."

8

I'm not sure I really had a choice, and If I did, I wasn't sure she would have waited for me to make it. Before I knew it, the room disappeared, and we were back out in the clearing. I felt the sun from the unseasonably warm day baking down on me, but that was it. The rest of the world was still, or make that frozen.

"Now, I am going to release your memory a little at a time," Mrs. Saxon said from behind me, where she and Samantha were playing hide and seek. "Just let it go, but tell me what you feel." She approached me, her voice growing nearer with each word, and then she walked in front of me. "I will see what you see, but I cannot feel what you feel. I need you to tell me, so I know when to stop. Okay?"

I guess. It wasn't like I could answer her if it wasn't. She placed her hands against my temples, like she had before, and the world slowly came to life. A light breeze passed by, and then it picked up a little brisker. It carried the precious laugh of my daughter, which at first sounded like it was in slow motion, but then took on its normal cherub tone. I watched as my hands moved, and then an image appeared in my head. A symbol. Wait no, two runes combined, very poorly might I add, but what were they. Everything paused again with the image in my head.

"Now, what is that?" Mrs. Saxon wondered aloud.

Two runes combined, I thought, hoping she could hear me.

"I see."

She could. That was good to know.

"But why? Why would anyone do that, and what symbols are they?"

It was something my father did. I read about it in his journals and did a little experimenting on my own. It allows you to...

"Combine the power of two or more runes," Mrs. Saxon completed my thought, and then had one of her own. "Fascinating," she said with all the wonder of a child that just saw a bird flying for the first time.

Now I just need to figure out what the two symbols were.

"I might have an idea," replied Mrs. Saxon. In a flash, I saw the lunar spiral appear all on its own. Then it came to me, and since she was reading my thoughts, Mrs. Saxon knew what I saw as well.

"It's crude, but yes, that was it. The lunar spiral and the chalice."

A chalice appeared below her lunar spiral, but she kept them separate, with lots of space between them. Mine were together, and crudely done.

"I probably couldn't have combined them better myself, but they are interesting choices. Both sources of what makes a woman a woman, and taps into her abilities of procreation, and," then she stopped.

What?

"Intuition, and psychic abilities," finished Mrs. Saxon. "I'm sure you have heard stories about mothers that felt something bad had happened to their child. Those aren't just stories. Those are true intuition and psychic connections through the strong emotional bounds we form with those we care about. They may be far away, but we can still feel them. Those symbols tap into both abilities and enhance them."

She paused, and I was about to ask what was next when she said, "Let's take another step." We did. I wish I could repeat that step for the rest of my life. Oh my god, the peace I felt was unlike anything I had ever felt in my life. I could have lived in this moment forever. It would be ironic if this grand peace caused my overload. An overdose of peace. Just my luck. Maybe I am a child of chaos.

Mrs. Saxon found that thought rather humorous and could barely contain herself, letting a chuckle slip through. "I doubt this was it, but I can feel the influence of the runes. The clarity and focus they brought you. Let's keep going."

Do we really have to?

There was no answer, but I could tell we were moving again. Then I felt something coming. At first, it was way far away, but it was speeding toward me.

"I think this is it."

It was like being in a car crash you knew was coming. I saw it coming. I couldn't avoid it, and I damn well knew it was going to hurt. I just couldn't prepare myself for how badly it was going to hurt.

There it was. Two words. Loud and clear in Nathan's own voice. "Help me!"

Did I say car wreck? This was an airplane crashing into a passenger train that I was riding the front of. The world around me broke down slowly, bit by bit, but the calm and tranquility went away in a flash of heat that seared every nerve in my body, before leaving me in a cold frozen nothingness. Then it stopped. Everything stopped, and unlike before, Mrs. Saxon's voice wasn't there to fill the void.

Did you hear it?

There was no response.

Mrs. Saxon? Did you hear it?

"Yes," she finally said, then we were back in my room. Mrs. Saxon stood up off the bed, and walked away from me, keeping her back to me. Her head slumped.

"He's in trouble!" I fell to the floor on my knees. Now feeling all the panic and pain I must have felt earlier to cause my overload. She held up a hand behind her to stop me from continuing.

"Let's not jump to any conclusions."

It was a good thing she could no longer read my thoughts, or she would have seen where all had jumped, and it was only about conclusions. I had already jumped to several hundred conclusions. I had also jumped on her for being so dismissive about her son crying out for help.

"That could have many meanings." She finally turned around toward me. How calm her face looked surprised me. This was her son we were talking about. "And they aren't anywhere close to the ones you are thinking of. With both of your heightened emotional states and the enhancement of your psychic abilities from those two runes, that could have been as much as him joking to someone to help him climb up on something or anything else rather innocent. Your state, with those amplifiers, would have made it feel more dire."

"It didn't just feel that way! It sounded it!" I leaned hard in her direction, and almost fell on my face, catching myself at the last moment. What the hell was wrong with her? This was her own son.

She held her arms up, almost defensively, and motioned for me to calm down. "Larissa, let me explain something about psychic connections. This was your first time experiencing it and you need to understand some principles. First, in most instances, time is irrelevant to the connection. What you sense, see, or hear could have happened yesterday, a year ago, and sometimes, they may have not happened yet. It's not a direct connection to that person right at that moment. Second, the emotions you feel are your own, just transferred to what you see or hear. Third, rarely do you receive anything that is complete. A feeling, a word, or a vision is just that. Part of a whole, which you don't see. Take it as just that. Of course, you heard Nathan appear to reach out for help, but that could be from an event you already had with him, or something rather innocent, like I said. Your powerful feelings for him. That deep concern you feel for him painted that message in a certain way, and that is how you took it. We shouldn't read anything into it."

"What?" I screamed, finding myself in a rare state, speechless. I couldn't believe what I was hearing.

"Considering the two runes you combined to enhance your abilities and the quick switch from calm to hysterical, it's no wonder your system went into overload." She placed both hands on her hips and said, "Well, I'm glad we figured that out. Now, you and I need to talk more about what your father was working on and what you remember from those journals. That is absolutely fascinating."

She approached the door, but stopped short of it. I was curious if she was going to actually go through it. No one other than Marie had come in or out of that door since I returned, and when that happened, we were extremely careful to make sure the hallway was clear. Her hand reached for the door handle, increasing my curiosity and I wondered if I should say something, but she stopped and turned back to me.

"But that is something for another time." Then she let go of the door handle and spun her hand around, opening one of her own, and walked toward it, almost cheery, with a bounce in her steps. That lit a short fuse on the bomb inside me. There was already a fuse burning from its other side, set by some of her earlier comments, and both just ran out. I bolted, cutting her off, just barely. My back was against the portal, and I was face to face with her, with only a few inches separating us. "What... About... Nathan?"

She didn't even flinch at the question. Her eyes kept steady contact with my own, and there wasn't even a blink. "That is something for another time." A force moved me aside, and she walked through the portal. It closed before I could follow, and I pounded my fist against the wall that was behind it.

9

I was still pounding on the door when a portal behind me opened up. I heard it and felt it, and was ready for Mrs. Saxon or someone to admonish my making so much noise.

"Mom, what's wrong?" Samantha asked from behind me, and I stopped my fists before they made their next strike.

"Nothing, I'm just a little mad." That was a lie. I was furious. I leaned forward and rested my forehead against the wall. In doing so, I caught a glimpse of myself in the mirror. A horror movie scene looked back at me. Eyes bulging and fangs out. All I needed to complete the picture was drool or foam dripping from the corners of my mouth. I didn't want her to see me that way, and I also wasn't sure if I could pull it together before I turned around, at least not naturally. A quick wave of my hand over my face fixed that. Thankfully, Mrs. Tenderschott's shake had some punch left in it. "Just a little mad. That is all." I tried to hide my inner madness and turned around.

"Mad about what?" asked Samantha.

Leave it to me to have an inquisitive child. Of course, I have heard all children are inquisitive. "It doesn't matter," I said, brushing it off in the hopes she will drop it, but doing so made me feel sick. Of course, it mattered. It was everything.

"Oh, alright."

The look on her face made me cringe. Wheels were turning inside her. She wasn't going to drop it as simple as I had hoped. Hopes were for fools. The cynic inside me knew that.

"Did you and Mrs. Saxon figure out what caused you to fall?" Samantha asked. She stood there with her hands folded in front of her, rocking back and forth on her sneakers.

"Yep." I nodded.

"What was it?"

"Let's just say magic is dangerous, and you shouldn't go playing with something you don't understand. I did, and you saw what happened to me."

Technically, I wasn't wrong. I was playing with something I didn't fully understand, but it wasn't the first time that had happened, and it probably wouldn't be the last. That seemed to be the best way to learn. Did I know those two runes would enhance those abilities? Yep, of course I did. By that much, maybe, or maybe not. That was not the problem. It was all about what I heard, and nothing could have prepared me for that. Even if I had the perspective and experience that Mrs. Saxon described, hearing Nathan cry out like that still would have floored me. Of that I had no doubt. Something inside me didn't buy her explanation. It just didn't feel right, and it smelled worse than the jars over on the table.

"That is why it is important to practice under the supervision of a teacher, understand?"

"Yes, I do." Samantha ran over and hugged me. This hug was no longer one around my legs. Her arm wrapped tightly around my stomach and her head was buried in her chest. I supposed most children, or maybe I would be better off calling her a pre-teen now, would hear the beating of their mother's heart when being held like this. There was no such luck for my child. She won't even hear my lungs fill with air. Which at this moment was a good thing. I was still seething inside, despite my calm exterior mirage.

"Did you have a good time with Mrs. Tenderschott?"

Samantha let go of me and backed up against the bed. She was beaming. "The best. Another student came in after I arrived. Not a witch. Maybe my age or younger. Mrs. Tenderschott had baked some cookies earlier. We ate them while she showed me a few potions."

"Another student?" I asked, knowing darn well Mrs. Tenderschott knew our presence needed to be kept a secret. Why would she allow another student in when Samantha was there? Mrs. Saxon had my blood boiling. This turned it to steam.

"Yes, her name was Amy. She's a shifter."

I turned right around to the wall and spun my arm, but nothing happened. A quick glance over my shoulder considered the tray of jars. There were only three left. I had been downing them with regularity lately. Without a second thought, I stomped over to the tray.

"Mom, where were you trying to go?" Sam asked.

"Oh, your mother needs to have a chat with Mrs. Tenderschott."

My hand had just touched the jar when Samantha stood up and said, "Let me help you."

Right there in front of me, my little girl opened a portal to Mrs. Tenderschott's classroom, and I had a feeling this wasn't her first. Someone, her grandmother, I think, had been working with her.

"Thank you." I walked over and kissed her on the forehead. "Now can you do me one more favor and go through it and make sure there is no one else in there?"

Samantha walked right through her own portal and looked around. I heard Mrs. Tenderschott address her, rather surprised just before Samantha announced, "It's all clear, mom."

That was my clue to storm through. The portal closed once I exited into the classroom. I wanted Samantha to go back and wait in our room, but she didn't, and it was too late now. The eruption was starting, and nothing would hold this back.

"What are you doing allowing other students to see Samantha?" I demanded, looking right at a stunned Mrs. Tenderschott. "No one is to know we are here."

"It's fine. I was here and made sure your secret stayed safe. She only knows that Sam is a young witch visiting the coven. The daughter of one of the council members that are temporarily housed here. Which is the way it ought to be if you ask me." She gave me a little wink and a smirk to diffuse the storm she knew was brewing inside.

"Samantha, can you head back to our room, please? Me and Mrs. Tenderschott need to talk." I never looked back at my daughter, keeping my attention right at the person whose judgment I was now questioning for the first time.

"Sure," responded Samantha.

The glow of her portal reflected off the walls in front of me. When it disappeared, I let my true self out.

"What the hell were you thinking?" I blasted, hoping her better judgement would show up and apologize for what I saw as a true lapse in her thought process.

"She is truly amazing. Mastering her abilities at such a young age. Even at the age of what she looks to be."

"Thanks," the proud parent inside of me stepped up and interrupted my rant for a moment, but only a brief one. "What were you thinking?"

"I was thinking there would be no harm as long as Amy didn't know who she really was," Mrs. Tenderschott explained, sounding a lot calmer than I did asking the question.

"No harm? No one is to know we are here. It's that simple. All someone has to do is start asking questions about the new person they met, and start putting two and two together and…" And, I wasn't sure what was next. I was even thinking I might have gone a little overboard here. I wasn't so sure Mrs. Saxon would agree, though. This was her rule, and she was very explicit about it.

"You are worrying about nothing. No one, and I mean no one, is going to connect a new witch here to being your child, or anything to do with you. There are only a few people here that even knew you were pregnant, and most of them don't know you already gave birth. Let alone. All of them, except a small circle of people, believe you are on the run after your miraculous escape from Mordin… Which you should have seen Mrs. Wintercrest's face when she announced that. I had never seen someone turn so red before. Her head was about to pop open like an overripe tomato."

"It doesn't matter, and Amy of all people… wait, how mad was she?" Hearing that I might have irritated someone that I can say I truly detested had my attention. Mrs. Tenderschott may have found the way to defuse the bomb inside me.

"Oh, she was spitting mad. She called everyone in before the council and stood up from her chair. Her hands trembled as she did her best to look in control, but we could all see how upset she was. She said you broke out, then broke Marcus Meridian out, and made a point to say they didn't understand how, but were sure it had something to do with you being a vampire. She called you a menace and danger to our world, which you need to know not a single member of the faculty believes. Then she told us that if any of us hears from you, or hears any news of you, we are to inform the council immediately. Larissa, I have to tell you. I have never seen a person so angry before. A werewolf, yes, but not a person. Her voice must have cracked a dozen or more times, and during my interview, she couldn't control the trembling."

"I'm shocked the old-bitty didn't have a heart attack... Wait? What? Your interview?"

"Yes, my interview. She and Miss Roberts interviewed the entire staff about the incident and your whereabouts. Not a soul said anything, and we never would."

Interview? The inferno that roared inside me froze over and I felt a chill go down my spine. I should have suspected they would question everyone in the coven. Why wouldn't they? I escaped from the unescapable. They had to assume I had help, regardless of how she may have believed it happened.

Her explanation of how it happened made no sense at all. My powers as a vampire. Please. Vampires can't fly. If I had broken out of my cage, something that was virtually impossible to do, I was sure I could have survived the fall to the ledge below me. That part was plausible, but exactly how did I find and rescue Marcus? The only rational explanation was I had help, which I did. They had to know that. They would also assume that help came from this coven, which again, it did. About a dozen people here knew the truth. Some wouldn't be able to protect themselves from the memory intrusion of the council. The vampires. My stomach tossed as I asked, "Everyone?"

"If you're asking if they interviewed Mrs. Saxon, but of course they did." She walked toward me and placed her hand on my shoulder. I expected her to pull me in for a hug. A very Mrs. Tenderschott thing to do, but she held me there and looked right into my eyes. She was very... well... parental at that moment. "You have nothing to worry about. She has plenty of tricks up her sleeve. She even used them to help the Boldens. No one knew a thing. Your secret will remain safe. Larissa, you have nothing to worry about. You have never had anything to worry about here."

I felt a little better and added a question for Mrs. Saxon about how to block those kinds of intrusions in the future to my list of things I wanted to learn. There was still something bothering me. It was what brought me here in the first place.

"Okay, but why Amy? Why put her in that situation?"

"Oh Larissa." Now she pulled me in for that big bear hug of hers. "What happened to the crass risk taker I knew? You are worried about nothing. No one is going to interview her. There are so many new people walking around with the council here, no one knows who is here or who isn't. Like I said, I told Amy she was the daughter of one of our visitors. That is it. Not to mention it is good for Samantha to be around people her own age," Mrs. Tenderschott paused at that and finally released me. "Or close to her own age," she said with a wry smirk. "She's spending way too much time with you old people." She chuckled and released me and headed for her front table where there was a plate with a half-eaten cookie on it and several sets of glasses and beakers. "I don't count. Remember, you are older than I am. So, how old do you believe she is now?" Mrs. Tenderschott asked as she cleaned off the table.

"Yesterday, probably eight or nine. Today maybe eleven. I'm losing track." I really was. Some days it seemed she stayed the same age for a while. Others, it seemed she skipped a year or two. I wasn't sure where it would stop. I hoped it would. I didn't want to face what it meant if it didn't. I was too worried about missing moments with her while my mind was obsessed elsewhere.

"That's kind of what I think too," she agreed. "You know her magic is progressing quickly. She is easily equal to most of the students here in general understanding, and I heard Master Thomas has even taught her some combat training." She placed the last beaker on the shelf it came from. Then she disposed of the half-eaten cookie by finishing it herself before putting the plate in the sink.

I joined her up at the table. There was no danger in doing that this time, as there was no potion waiting for me. "How's Amy?"

"She is doing wonderfully. She isn't a witch, but I check in on her from time to time." Mrs. Wintercrest washed the crumbs off the plate down the drain of the sink, and with her back to me said, "You know Laura picked up reading to her every night." Mrs. Tenderschott choked on those words and looked over her shoulder to see if I was cringing. I wasn't, much. As much as I missed doing that with Amy, I was happy to hear someone had picked it up for her. "Of course, you wouldn't," she nervously corrected herself while fidgeting with her dish towel before folding it and placing it next to the sink, but keeping her hand on it. "You are isolated from the other vampires as well, aren't you?"

"Yes," I said, rather curious why she didn't know that.

"I wasn't sure considering..." Mrs. Tenderschott turned away from me. The woman was flat hiding something from me and that had me concerned. It was so unlike the woman I knew as the gossip queen around here.

"Considering what?"

Boy, I didn't really understand what that question would bring. It was as if the Hoover Dam gave way and the Colorado River stormed through. With a whirl, the dish towel went flying, as did her hands and her curly gray hair. "Oh Larissa, it's all a huge mess," she blurted. "They isolated the vampires away from the witches at the order of the council. Separate classes and everything. No one here knows about what is going on out there. At least none of the students do, but the council didn't want to take any chances, so they ordered the split, and *that* was a positive outcome." She slammed her hand down on the table in front of the room. "Originally, they wanted to exile them all. That wicked... whatever she is... wanted to kick them all out in the cold. Rebecca argued over and over how they had nothing to do with any of this and it would be cruel. None of that meant anything to that heartless wench of a supreme and her little mini-me Miss Roberts." Mrs. Tenderschott was practically spitting. Her finger wagged in the air, trying to keep up with every point. "It was only when Rebecca told them that turning them out would just turn them against all witches and aid the vampires that Mrs. Wintercrest," she said. That name appeared bitter to her tongue. "She *decided* it would be better to keep them here imprisoned until all this is settled and *then* they could be released out into the wild, as she said. Can you believe she used that description? It's like she is talking about releasing some kind of wild animal. It's a horrible bloody mess created by the council, and for what? I don't have a freckle of a clue."

"Wait! Wait! Wait! Come again?"

"They keep the vampires and witches separate from everyone. In fact, they keep everyone separate from the witches. The shifters, werewolves, and vampires are not permitted to be around the witches." She held up a finger and pursed her lips. "Wait here."

She rushed back through the door that I knew led to her apartment. I heard her go through another door inside there, and then it slammed shut. It wasn't more than a few seconds before she emerged from her apartment. Her hand held out a gold chain in front of her. Dangling from that chain was a charm, or make that a symbol, a solar cross.

"They charmed these and made all the witches wear them to protect us from the others. It causes pain to any non-witch that comes close to us."

I stepped back, not knowing what it would do to me since a part of me wasn't a witch, and Mrs. Tenderschott nodded her approval at my action. Then she tossed the chain on a table on the other side of the classroom. It slid across the surface and stopped just short of the edge.

"From what I have heard, it's quite painful. Gwen wasted no time in trying it out on Apryl. It sent the poor girl to the floor. Everyone has scattered and kept their distances since then." She looked at the shiny object on top of the black tabletop on the other side of the room with disdain. "I don't wear it unless the council is around. Demius is trying to counteract the spell on it, but so far, he hasn't been able to."

"Oh Jesus. This is bad. This is terrible." I repeated it a few more times, while the list of people's lives I had screwed up rushed through my head. That list was about to reach across oceans. I had always thought it was just a cliché in the movies when someone who was panicking said the room was spinning. Now I was either living that cliché or it was real. The room spun around me, and I felt my knees grow weak. I backed up into the table behind me, sending it screeching across the floor. My hand covered my mouth, but it was too late, and it slipped out. "It's all my fault."

"Now you stop that right now." Mrs. Tenderschott stormed toward me. "You stop that right now. This is all the council's doing."

I heard what she said, but I also didn't. This had nothing to do with the council. This was all my doing. All of it. Every single bit of it. I couldn't list anything that had happened that didn't start with me. If Mrs. Saxon was right, and she saw everything that was going to happen, why didn't she leave me on the train?

"Stop," she said as she reached under my chin and tilted my head up. "Just stop. This is all the council's doings. They have been wanting to do this for years, probably centuries. You need to stay focused, because you are the one that is going to fix all of this."

"Wait!" Hearing that come from her sent shockwaves through me. "You know?"

"Please. I've always known. I was there when Rebecca talked to Benjamin about it."

"Man, is anything a secret around here?" I scoffed.

"Well, there are a few. Your presence is one. Then there is your daughter, Marie Norton, Marcus, and Jack and Lisa." Mrs. Tenderschott counted it off on her fingers, and then held up her hand so I could see five fingers.

I knew of three of those five, but two of the names were a shock. "Jack and Lisa? What's their secret?"

"Their existence," Mrs. Tenderschott answered before walking away toward the table with her what I would call cursed charm laying on it. "The council doesn't know they are here. Which is why I felt it was okay for them to be around you the other day, and why they don't have one of those blasted things." She glanced over at the chain on the table. "Rebecca is concerned... rightly so, that someone might recognize those two from the fight down in New Orleans and would remember they weren't exactly fighting on the side of the witches. So, they are stuck off on their own."

Oh yeah. I remembered Mrs. Saxon mentioning she was keeping them separate from the other witches, but she said it was to protect my secret from getting out, not to protect them. Then I realized who she was trying to protect.

"You don't need to worry about that, though. You have enough to focus on, like your daughter–"

"And my training." I interrupted with the obvious answer.

"Yes, your training. Speaking of, how is that going?"

"A little better now, thanks to your potions. I might need some more or something stronger."

"How many do you have left?" she asked in a curious tone.

"Three." I held up three fingers.

Now it was her turn to be shocked. "Three? As in one, two, three?" She counted off on her own fingers.

"Yep, they are working great."

"Larissa, I just gave you those two days ago. It's supposed to be one a day, at the most."

Oops. All I could do was shrug. "It's not like there was a prescription label on them with instructions." I tried to remember if she said anything about how often I should take it. I couldn't remember any instructions besides using them to help me with my training sessions. Perhaps she assumed one per day would suffice. It probably would have if I hadn't taken part in some extracurricular activities.

"Trying a few things on your own?" she asked with a suspicious look in her eye.

"Just practicing." It wasn't a wrong answer. I was practicing. What I was practicing was going to stay my secret. "It has helped a lot. Thank you." I hoped my show of humbled gratitude would change that subject, but the look she gave me didn't change. "It even lets me throw some runes."

Now it changed to one of surprise. "Really? It helped you become that focused?"

"Yes." I nodded, "but it backfired. I think I tapped into something I wasn't ready for and..." As I explained what happened, a question came to me. A nagging I had felt since Mrs. Saxon explained to me what I had experienced and how easily she blew off any concerns for Nathan, fueled its origins. "Can I ask you something? It's about the runes I tried and what seemed to have backfired."

"Yes, of course." Mrs. Tenderschott settled up against the table in front of her and had a seat. She tapped her hand on the tabletop, summoning me to sit across from her. I didn't resist and took a seat. "So, what's the question?"

"The rune I chose tapped into some psychic abilities." I didn't want to get into the entire explanation with her about how my father combined symbols to create new ones and that I did the same with two that were involved with psychic connections while not even understanding what psychic connections were. That was a topic for another time, to borrow Mrs. Saxon's statement from earlier. Not to mention I wanted to avoid any type of lecture I might get about being careless with magic. "It was my first time doing that."

"Oh, then you absolutely weren't ready for it. Psychic connections and impulses are powerful. You need to develop a filter to keep it from overloading your own system."

So much for avoiding a lecture. "No kidding. That's what happened."

She reached over and took my hand. The chill of my touch never deterred her from showing me the same warm affection that she showed everyone else, and I always appreciated that. She treated me and the rest as if we were just people. "Good lord. Please tell me Rebecca was there to intervene."

"She was. She froze me and brought me back to my room until I recovered. Then we went through something that took us step by step so she could see what caused it."

"Good. She did the right thing. I have to tell you, if she wasn't there, it could have been damaging to you," warned Mrs. Tenderschott. "You need to be careful about trying new things on your own. Even someone as experienced and capable as you are can step into something you aren't ready for."

"That's what I need to ask you about. I want to make sure I understand what happened. When I was in what you and Mrs. Saxon called a psychic connection, I heard or felt something. That was the moment I became overloaded." I leaned forward. "When you are in that state, and you feel emotions in what you are... I guess... receiving is the right word, are those just your emotions reacting?"

"Well, yes, of course. Your emotions are going to react to what you see, hear–"

"Oh, good." I interrupted her, feeling relieved, but not realizing I just talked over a very important part of her answer until she finished it.

"–and feel. Emotions are particularly important in those connections. You need to understand what you feel while being able to control the flood you are receiving. The emotions that travel across the connection are raw and stronger than anything we feel ourselves."

My head did a double take, and I almost leaped across the table at the woman. What did she just say? "You mean the emotions you feel are real? They're really what the person you have the connection with is feeling?"

"Of course, silly," she said as if it were something obvious that everyone knew. "The psychic connection between two or more people is an extremely powerful connection, fueled mostly by emotions. That is why it is important to learn how to filter most of it out and let just a little through. Those emotions you receive are raw and very strong."

"That..." I muttered, catching myself before I called Mrs. Saxon something that even she didn't deserve. She lied to protect me. I let go of Mrs. Tenderschott's hand and propped my head on my left hand while my right one clawed at the table.

"Larissa, what is it?"

There was a momentary debate about whether I should tell her. When my mouth finally opened, I had either forgotten, or just ignored, all the reasons I shouldn't tell her. The first sound that made it out was a sob, then the words followed. "When I was under, I heard Nathan cry out for someone to help. It was just two words, 'help me', but they were strong, and the desperation consumed me. Mrs. Saxon told me those were my emotions, transplanted on top of what I heard." Now I knew different and that same desperation I felt while in the connection threatened to swallow me again.

"What did he say? What did you see?" Both questions fired from her lips. Now it was her turn to lean across the table, eager for my reply.

"Just 'help me'. I saw nothing. It was more about what I felt."

Mrs. Tenderschott stood up and stumbled away from the table. She had something to say, but struggled to find either the breath or words. When she did, there was an attempt to compose herself, and it only half succeeded. "He's alive. That's good."

"Well, he may be alive," I said. It was a statement that almost broke me in half, but I had to face the possibility.

"No. If you heard him, he is alive. What you hear is what is happening at that moment."

"What?" I jumped off of my stool and leaned hard over the table, supporting myself with both of my arms. "She told me that time was irrelevant!"

There was a quick and surprised shake of her head. "No, that is incorrect. What you see or hear is happening at that moment." Then she wondered aloud, "She knows that. I wonder why she…", but she never finished the thought.

I wasn't sure if I had steam coming out of my ears, but I should have. I was fuming and ready to go to war on my own. She lied to me. Yes, I wasn't too blinded by rage and concern to know she did it to protect me from, well, me. She knew what I would do if I knew the truth.

It seemed Mrs. Tenderschott knew too. She rushed toward me. "Larissa, don't do anything rash. I know what it seems like, but it could have many meanings."

"Now you sound exactly like her," I snapped and walked away. "You have already told me the truth. What I felt was what he was feeling at *that* time. I'm not sure how many other meanings that could have. He was in trouble and in severe pain. Both physically and emotionally." I turned to look at her, and half cried, and half screamed, "He was hurt and crying out for someone to help." My voice echoed around the classroom as I reached up to brush away the tears running down my cheeks. "And that," I left what I was really thinking out after a second of discretion, "she just ignored it. Her own son!" I paced around the classroom like a caged animal, which wasn't all that wrong.

"Now, now, Larissa. I know that is what it looks like, but I seriously doubt that." There was an edge to her voice that took some of the consolation out of it. She was both irritated and concerned. "You need to remember something about Rebecca. She is reserved and calculated. She has to be. It is required of her position, and it is just how her nature is. You are more emotional. I assure you. She is not turning a blind eye to her son and is working on something to help him." She stammered with her explanation.

She might be right, but how long would she wait before she took action? If it were me, I would have gone to him immediately. Well, there was the minor problem of not knowing where he was. A problem that had a solution waiting for me in the books in my room. I had to believe Mrs. Saxon probably already knew how to do those spells, and being his mother, she had more options to choose from. I only had one, and I was starting on that as soon as I got back to my room.

"I'm going to need more of that stuff you gave me to focus."

"I can't," responded Mrs. Tenderschott. She held up a hand defensively as I paced toward her, and it caught me off guard. Had I frightened her that much?

"Before you think I am saying I won't. It's not that. I can't. I'm out of a few key ingredients. They take about a week to make." When she lowered her hand, I saw a faint glow I hadn't seen before. She honestly thought I was coming at her. "I know what you are planning to do with it, and it is a bad idea. Your magic isn't stable right now. You shouldn't be going off anywhere until that problem is solved."

She appeared to have more to say, but I didn't let her. "But Nathan is the answer to that problem! Don't you see?"

"Wait," she responded, and I put the rest of my speech on hold. "I understand that. I truly do. I figured it was that as soon as you started struggling, but Larissa, you can't go out into the middle of a war like this. You can't defend yourself."

"Then fix me something to help," I roared, and felt bad about it as soon as my mouth shut. Not that it made up for it, I added, "Please."

"I can't. There is nothing I can make that will help. For your own good. You need to calm down and think things through. You are in no shape to help Nathan. I'm sure Rebecca is working on something."

10

Mrs. Tenderschott proved her point by having me try to open a portal back to my room, and there wasn't even a fizzle of anything as I spun my arm around. She opened it for me and sent me back through with a hug, a kiss on the cheek, and orders to sit tight and let Mrs. Saxon handle things. Sit tight in my room and do nothing. That was highly unlikely. I just needed to figure out what I was going to do, and, most importantly, how I was going to do it. I only had three jars left, and as much as I wanted to use one now, my better judgment spoke up through my raging emotions and convinced me to hold off until I really needed it.

Samantha was already asleep when I came through, and I stayed quiet to keep from waking her. It was early, but I had a feeling today's events with her mom causing a scene, falling and all, had tired her out. I motioned for the books to go over to my desk, but they didn't. Not even a budge or a jerk. I had to move them in a more conventional manner.

As I walked over to pick them up, I passed by the window in my room and paused for just a second to look out. I had done that often since I had returned. Until Master Thomas arranged our field trips, that was the only view Samantha, or I, had of the outside world. I rarely looked out the window at night. Mostly because it was dark, and I wouldn't be able to see as far. Being winter, there seemed to be a constant cloud cover, blocking any brilliant moonlit nights.

I don't know why I did it this time. Then again, maybe I did. Maybe it was what Mrs. Tenderschott told me. I looked down at the table Nathan and I used to sit at to read to Amy. There they were: Amy and Laura. Amy held the book and appeared to be reading to Laura. I was a little surprised not to see Mike out there. Then again, maybe I wasn't. This was more her thing. It brought a smile to my face, but also tugged at my heart. I wanted to be down there. Scratch that. I needed to be down there. I glanced back at Samantha, to remind myself that I had mine. Maybe this was Laura's chance to have hers. That was when something she said back in New Orleans made sense, and I felt bad that I didn't fully understand until now. Laura wanted a child. Something our state robbed us of, or should have. God, she probably hated me when this happened to me. Thinking back to a few of the looks she gave me; I think she did.

I still had every intention of Amy being Samantha's big sister. Make that her sister. I think Samantha had already passed Amy's age. I so wanted them to have that connection, but could I break up what she was developing with Laura? Did I even have too? We were all one big extended family, and the werewolves were the crazy uncles. As I looked down upon them, and how closely they sat to one another, with no Ms. Parrish watching from a distance, I had to wonder if Amy felt for Laura how she did me?

No, you can't do that yourself. I had to give myself that quick lecture and move away from the window. I wasn't being replaced. That wasn't what was going on. I could still be part of her life, and everything was going to be fine. No matter how many times I tried to imagine that picture of the perfect family, Nathan, me, Samantha, and Amy, the feeling that someone had replaced me crept in. Every so often, a question would follow it. Was it all for the best? I wasn't totally sure how I felt about that question yet.

Before any of that picture could come true, I needed to deal with the first member who was missing. I needed a plan. Something I didn't usually rely on, at least until our plan to lure Jean St. Claire into an altercation in New Orleans. Before that, I always just acted and dealt with what came. It wasn't exactly the best way to go about things, but it had worked so far. Things were different now, and I wasn't really in a condition to just go in some place with both barrels blasting. My barrels were now nothing more than popguns and I didn't really know where I was going. That was problem number one, and a timely reminder of what I was doing when I stopped at the window.

I grabbed all seven books, a rather large stack that I had to peer over the top of, as I carried them to the desk. I almost dropped them on the top of the desk, but I remembered I had a daughter sleeping just a few feet away. So, I opted for a less noisy move, and placed them down gently on the desk. Little puffs of dust escaped from between the pages as the weight of each book settled on the one below it. A sign that no one in this place had looked into these topics in a long while, if ever. Not a shock, but also a reminder of how on my own I was here.

Book one was where I wanted to start again, and it was easy to find the page I needed thanks to the dogear I folded into the top edge earlier. Sorry Edward. "Blood of my Blood". Out of all the methods I'd read, this was the most direct. According to the text, I needed a hair or some biological trace of the person we were trying to find, or the blood from one of their direct descendants. The stronger the relationship, the better. There were warnings about not going beyond first cousins. That far out, it would be shaky, and you might find the location of half your family tree in the process. That wasn't a problem for me. I had exactly what I needed. You couldn't get much closer.

An old question arrived just in time to shake my confidence on that matter. How much was our daughter really our daughter, and how much of her had been created by magic? It is entirely possible there was no biological part of Nathan in her. Not knowing how she really came to be was a problem. My hand squeezed the edge of the book harder. It seemed everywhere I turned there were questions, and not a single answer, but this was one I could finally answer. If this worked, assuming I perform the spell and potion correctly, then I would have my answer. One way, or the other.

I kept reading through all the variations of this spell for the main spell and potion. Why you put variations before the main content, I didn't understand. It was a bad book design, in my opinion, but then again, most of the magical teachings I had been through weren't exactly forthright. You had to try it and figure it out as you went.

Then, like a shotgun blast to my soul, "Help me. Please!"

It seared right through me and sent me tumbling out of my chair to the floor.

"Please!" his voice begged again, echoing in my head. More intense than the previous plea. I reached out for him, and he wasn't there. I spun around and searched the entire room. I knew it was hopeless. I knew he wasn't there. I felt it. His voice was as distant as it was desperate, but the feelings were right there with me. It was as if we shared our being, and were one, both feeling what the other felt. Which was a horrifying realization for both of us. If I felt his suffering this strongly, then he felt what it did to me. He felt that hole. That empty void that grew by the moment. He felt me tumbling into it each time I realized what he was going through. I tried to convince myself I needed to be strong for him. I needed to be strong for myself and use that strength to find him. It was a grand idea, and I even had a great speech that went with it, but that didn't stop me from sitting there on the floor rocking back and forth and sobbing for hours before I finally climbed back into the chair.

When my mind finally focused on the page, I realized the spell itself didn't seem too hard on the surface. I had to hold the thought and feelings I have for my lost family member in my heart while I recited, "Blood of my Blood. Bound of my bound. Heart of my heart. Reach to me." In fact, it sounded downright corny. I then turned the page to the next part, which was the potion, which again, wasn't that hard. Just a few ingredients that I was sure Mrs. Tenderschott had in her classroom. But when I read the next instruction, and what I had to do, I about knocked the book to the floor in shock. I had to find a four-foot-by-four-foot piece of parchment paper and soak it with blood and potion, and it would draw a map to the person. Soak?!? I was thinking a little drop. This thing wants to me slit Samantha's throat and bleed her out over a large poster. No way in hell.

This had to be a mistake. I kept reading through the variations of the potion for less direct relationships, like siblings and grandparents, and finally reached the part about using a strand of hair instead of blood. There! That was my solution to all this. I probably would have to burn it or something. Easy enough, and I was right. You were to burn the strand and... wait, and then allow your astral self to follow the smoke to the person you seek. Ah crap! My head collapsed down on to the book when I read, "only to be used if the person was within a few miles of you." Great, I now knew how to find Samantha if I ever lost her at the mall, but this wouldn't work for what I needed. As far as I knew, he was thousands of miles away.

There had to be another way. The book was thick enough to be loaded with hundreds of ways to do this. I pushed myself back up, but disappointment weighed on my head so much I had to prop it up with my arm. I flipped the page, and it listed ingredients for the other potions which were not for direct relationships like father and child. Then down at the bottom in small italics there was a note. It said, "Spells you may also need—Congero." That was a word I had never seen before, let alone spell. I flipped through the book for a page covering this spell. Of course, that would make things easy, and as I had already noted, nothing in the world of witches was the easy way. We made triumphs through struggle. I could almost hear Master Thomas' voice echoing with that in my ears.

I spun around in the chair, shutting the book. I almost slammed it shut, but remembered my sleeping daughter and caught it before the pages clapped together. I scanned the room for two books. I knew they were in here. Mrs. Saxon gave them to me the first day I found out, or the first day she told me, I was a witch, again. If only I could remember where I left them. I gave the desk another quick glance, just to be sure. I didn't remember ever reading them at my desk. Where was I? Then it hit me, and I sprinted to my bed, where I always sat or laid while looking through Mrs. Saxon's Elemental Spells Volumes I and II. I never made it to volume II. I really only made it halfway through volume I before I remembered who I was, and all that came rushing back to me. So, I wasn't sure if Congero, or whatever it was called, was in there or not. I hoped it was. If not, it was back to the library, or a special request to Edward. But could I risk that? I knew he was reporting back to Mrs. Saxon. Would such a simple request tip either of them off to what I was doing? I looked around on the bed for the books, checking under the covers that I never used, and the same with the blanket folded at the foot of it. Nothing. Then, on a hunch, remembering how things would become lost in my room when I was a little girl, I reached down between my bed and the wall. Bingo! Two books. I made quick work fanning through volume I at a speed that created a slight breeze in the room that even I felt. I took more time going through volume II, having never read it before. When I hit the last page, I let it just fall limp with the others. Nothing. Not even a single mention of that spell as part of something else. This wasn't just a roadblock. This was a brick wall that extended up to the moon. I needed another witch's help.

The biggest question was who? Mrs. Saxon was an absolute no. I couldn't risk it. Not that she would understand what I was really doing. At least I didn't think so. Of course, if her divination was as good as she claimed it was, she would already know I was doing this. That begs the question, why wasn't she up here trying to stop me?

Master Thomas was a curious consideration. I wasn't sure if he would object to teaching me something new. He might push back on putting something else on my plate until I was controlling the simple things first. I'm sure he would probably ask why, and I would say because it was part of a spell I was reading about, and then he would ask what spell that was, and the dance would go on. Too exhausting, but he might be the only option. Mrs. Tenderschott was a no. I was almost sure she would report back to Mrs. Saxon. She was already concerned I was going to do something foolish. That didn't leave me with many options. It really left only one, but I wasn't thrilled by that prospect.

There was another option, but to say it was the riskiest of all wasn't stretching it.

11

With a head full of doubt, which wasn't exactly the optimal state to perform magic, I stood up and spun my arm around. Nothing. I forgot. See what an unfocused mind causes. For just a second, I considered waking Samantha to ask for her help, but I quickly dismissed that, and not for the obvious reason. I was certain she would say no. My eyes landed on the tray on the nightstand. There were only three jars left, and I needed to make them last. Mrs. Tenderschott said it would be another week before she could make more. Of course, I had a habit of rationalizing everything, so just a sip should be enough to get me where I was going and back, so that was what I did.

I popped up the top of one jar and powered through the putrid aroma that filled the room, and took a sip, which wasn't more than a drop or two. Samantha rustled in her bed, probably from the smell that I thought could wake the dead. While that quick sip tortured my throat, I tightly resealed the top on the jar and sat it back on the tray. Was this enough? There was only one way to find out.

I went to the far corner of the room, not wanting to wake Samantha, and tried again. This time I saw a familiar gold glitter portal open. On the other side was another room, and not just any room. It was the room of a very sleepy witch who was shielding her eyes from the bright, spinning disk. I stepped through, letting it close immediately, returning the room to complete darkness. Which didn't last long. Lisa flicked a candle on her nightstand after just a second or two.

She rolled over and groaned. "I'm not sure if I should be happy that you seem to have a better handle on your magic, or mad at you for waking me up. Vampires may not sleep, but the rest of us do." She rolled over facing me, gripping her covers tight.

"Sorry Lisa. I need your help with something, and it couldn't wait." Now that I had her attention. She sat up in the bed and appeared more awake.

"What is it?" she asked, concerned.

"I need you to ask a question for me," I started, and then stopped. Was I now questioning if I could trust Lisa? I had to trust someone, and Lisa was my best option. "I was looking up a potion, and it involved a spell I have never heard of. I tried to look it up, but I can't find any other references to it, and I need you to ask a teacher about it for me." I flashed my ever so convincing grin. "Could you do it?"

She rubbed her eyes and then asked. "Sure, but what's the spell? Maybe I have heard of it."

"Congero."

"That would be a big nope. Can you spell it?"

"C...O...N...G...E...R...O"

"Can you use it in a sentence?" she asked with a giggle. She leaned forward toward her desk, which was right next to her bed, and pulled two books off the black wood top.

"That would be a big nope."

She let go of her copies of Elementary Spell Volumes I and II, and sat back on the bed. "Already looked?"

I nodded. "It was the second place I looked after I checked the text I saw the reference in."

"Must be pretty advanced. Why can't you ask Mrs. Saxon or Master Thomas? I am sure one of them would know what it is."

A logical question that I knew she would ask. Now, if there were questions left about trusting Lisa, I needed to get over them. To borrow an old saying that I heard Mr. Norton say a few times, I was about to open the barn door and let all the animals out. Why I even questioned it? I didn't have a clue. Lisa was as close to a sister as I had. "I'm sure they do too, but they would ask why I wanted to know, and I sort of can't tell them."

"What are you planning?" Her worry from before was gone, and a mischievous smile stretched across her face. I knew this was coming. The barn door was open, and here came the animals.

"You can't tell a soul."

Lisa motioned she was locking her lips and throwing away the key.

I went over and sat beside her on the bed. "Remember when I first got here, and I was trying to find Marie?"

Lisa nodded.

"Well, Edward gave me some books on how to locate loved ones and then use astral projection to go find them, but warned me about how dangerous it was. I only looked through them once back then and set them aside. Now I have another use for them, and I found a spell and potion combination that might help me find Nathan."

"Wait, you aren't thinking of going to him in the astral plane, are you? Not only is that extremely dangerous. We only tried it, what, once, maybe twice? Larissa, you can't seriously be considering—"

I was sure Lisa had more points to make, but I didn't need to hear all the leaps she had made and put a single finger over her lips to hush her. "I'm not. This isn't this kind of spell and potion. This will draw a map to where he is, but there is a catch. I have to use a little blood from someone who is a direct relative of the person

I am searching for." I may have understated the amount of blood I needed, but that was intentional. "I am supposed to mix that with a few other ingredients and soak a large piece of parchment. Then say the spell while thinking of the person I am searching for, and it will draw a map to them on the parchment."

"Oh wow, do you think it will work?" she asked, wide-eyed.

"I guess," I responded with a shrug. "I just need to solve one problem. That large piece of parchment is really large. Like four-feet-by-four-feet, and if you think about what I told you, I need to soak it with Sam's blood." I didn't need to finish. The horrified look on Lisa's face said it all. She got my problem. "I'm hoping Congero has something to do with it."

"I'll ask during our private classes tomorrow." Lisa looked around the room for a minute and then suggested. "I can tell them it was something I read about. They won't suspect a thing."

I put my hands on my hips and cocked my head to the side.

"Right," she agreed.

"They wouldn't suspect a thing until you gave them that explanation. We all know no one goes to the library, and it's not in any of the assigned text or reading. Remember, they don't know I'm here visiting you right now, so they won't suspect anything."

But Lisa was right. If it is something special or some kind of restricted magic, they would be curious about where she heard about it. I had no clue how old those books were. Maybe it was like the runes. Something that wasn't supposed to be taught, but I had a way around that. Something that would sound both innocent and likely, considering her background. "Tell them you heard your mother speak of it before."

Lisa considered this for a second while lightly nodding. I think she realized the genius of my idea.

"So, you'll do it?" I asked eagerly.

"Of course," responded Lisa, without hesitation. "There is just one question. Once I find out what it is, how do I tell you?"

"That's easy." I raised my eyebrows a bit. "How did I come see you?"

"Oh yeah. I must be tired. My mind was thinking about our current restrictions, but that doesn't stop us," Lisa said, adding air quotes to the last two words.

"Once you have it, just come see me in my room. Deal?"

"Deal," agreed Lisa.

"Okay, I need to get back." My focus was on Lisa as I reached back and spun a portal open and stepped back through it. I should have known something was wrong. The telltale light it usually produced was rather dim, and Lisa's eyes were huge as she called my name just before I stepped through. It closed, leaving me standing in the middle of the hallway on the witch's floor. Worst of all, I heard voices coming from the commons room. One was an overly perky voice that sent chills down my spine.

Quickly, I attempted to open another portal, but nothing. Not even a fizzle. That sip hadn't lasted as long as I had hoped, and now I was in trouble and stuck on the other side of enemy lines, as some might see it. There were two choices. The door, which was a terrible idea. It lead to the stairs out in the grand entrance. Not exactly a place I wanted to walk if I intended to remain hidden. The other option was having Lisa help me, which was the obvious choice. My hand had already made that decision and was turning the handle on the door behind me.

"Dang it," I muttered. The room was dark and empty, completely empty. This wasn't Lisa's room. It wasn't anyone's room. I looked down the hall and saw Lisa's door. It was just two doors away. I thought of bolting for it, but the sound of Gwen's voice bleeding out from the commons room stopped me in my tracks. I heard other voices, but hers was the one that stuck out. Maybe it was how it grated against my nerves, but just hearing it made me feel ill, and my skin tingled, almost like it was burning. The feeling grew stronger, and her voice grew closer. She was coming out. I needed somewhere to hide, but the hallway was just that. A hallway with doors. I reopened the door I stood next to, and slipped inside, closing it as quietly as I could behind me.

I heard the sounds of footsteps as Gwen and whoever else was with her passed by, and the tingling I felt sent me to my knees on the floor. The tingling turned into a stabbing, like hundreds and hundreds of needles stabbing into my skin. Each hole burned on both entry and exit, and my body fell flat on the floor. There was no doubt I was feeling pain now. I reached up to push myself back up and saw my hand. My skin was just thin dry paper wrapped tightly around the bones of my fingers. I was afraid to move my fingers out of fear it would tear, but that didn't stop my reflexes from balling up my fingers into a fist with the next stabbing sensation. Then it was gone, along with the sound of footsteps. I laid there in the darkness and watched my hand return to normal. I could only assume the same happened to the rest of me.

What I felt had to be the stupid charms that the council gave all the witches. They were more powerful than I thought, and Mrs. Tenderschott left out one of their effects. Though she may not have known about it. There was a good chance none of the witches did either. How would they? They didn't see or hear the world as we do. They aren't able to hear the heartbeat of every living creature around them or smell that life giving fluid that coursed through their veins. I wasn't able to do either as they approached. I was sure Gwen wore hers around like a medal. Once the effects had passed, I stood up and cracked open the door. The hallway not only looked clear but also felt clear. There were no voices, and no sensations from the charms.

I made my way down the hallway, only feeling slight pinches and stabs from those who must have been close to their doors. This was the easiest part of my little journey. Just to be sure, I tried to open another portal, but nothing happened. Even an act as simple as drawing the all-seeing eye so I could see through the door was a big nothing. Something that should have frustrated me, but it instead struck me as humorous. Here I was panicking because I lost control of magic. I had forgotten all about my other side. The side that lived in the shadows. This should be easy. I would be out the door and up the stairs before anyone knew. This time of night, the lights would be down in the grand entry, anyway.

With a quick crack of the door, I checked to make sure no one else was out there on the stairs on our side or the boy's side. The coast was clear, and I made my way out to the stairs and sprinted up. The sound of an army thundered into the hall. I sped up, but then slowed down when I heard Mrs. Saxon's voice.

12

I felt them before I saw who they were, and not in the traditional way. The tingling and stabbing started before I saw them. Those damn charms. I moved up to the top landing and hid behind the thick wooden post. In hindsight, I should have made a break for the door. I could have been through it before anyone noticed. It would have saved me some torture, but it was too late now. At least where I was now had reduced the effects of the charms to nothing more than something like bug bites. Just an annoyance that caused my body to twitch. My hands rubbed up and down my legs and stomach to relief the itching, but that didn't work. I made another glance at the door. I was curious about who was coming, but was I really that curious?

My answer really didn't matter. Time had answered that question for me. I forced my body to stay still while I watched Mrs. Wintercrest and that thorn-in-my-side, Miss Roberts, lead the council marching by the stairs in rows of two. Each wore their ceremonial red robes. It was amazing. Even in something so regal, Miss Roberts looked tacky. I wasn't sure which witch I disliked most, Gwen or her. That was unfair. It was definitely her. I hated her, and I just disliked Gwen. If I were allowed to talk to the witches, I might plant a few suggestions in Gwen's head about Miss Roberts and see what trouble I could stir up.

"Council members, please," Mrs. Saxon's voice yelled from down the hall. She sounded out of breath. In a few seconds, her first step hit the marble floor of the entry, and the click of her heel echoed in the grand space. Ms. Wintercrest appeared to huff at the commotion. I felt a little pleasure at seeing her irritation. "Supreme Wintercrest, if I may?" she requested.

Mrs. Wintercrest never looked back in her direction, but her mini-me Miss Roberts stepped right out of the line and turned, blocking Mrs. Saxon's approach.

"You have made your point quite clear, Mrs. Saxon." Miss Roberts leered with a point of her finger right at Mrs. Saxon.

Mrs. Saxon ignored both her and her attitude without so much as a look and attempted to walk right around her. Miss Roberts shuffled to her right to block her. The two almost collided, and Mrs. Saxon had to give ground to avoid hitting her. I looked up and down the line of council members for any reaction. Most appeared to be ignoring what was going on. Even Mr. Nevers, who I knew well from my time in

New Orleans. He wasn't exactly a fan of Mrs. Wintercrest, and I couldn't imagine he was supportive of anything that was going on. Though I wasn't sure what type of reaction I expected from him or any of the other members. Mrs. Wintercrest had her thumb pressed tightly on each of them. That and the threat of exile I had already seen her use now twice. I believed that was why Mrs. Saxon dance carefully around her objections. "Just one more point, and that is all."

Finally, Mrs. Wintercrest turned, with her nose upturned, as if she were looking down on Mrs. Saxon. Something that was rather absurd, since Mrs. Saxon was a good foot taller than our diminutive supreme.

Miss Roberts stepped in front of Mrs. Saxon yet again and smiled smugly. But that expression didn't last long. Mrs. Wintercrest commanded her to move aside with a simple touch on her shoulder, and Miss Roberts complied immediately. She looked like someone had stolen her lollipop.

"Mrs. Saxon, we just spent an hour talking about this in council," started Mrs. Wintercrest. "Your attendance was a mere courtesy since we are here. Don't take your presence in those proceedings as meaning you have a say."

"I'm not, my supreme. I just believe there is a vantage point that wasn't considered or brought up. Just an omission, I'm sure."

"Probably, and it is probably not significant, or we would have discussed it. But since you interrupted us on the way to our quarters to retire for the night, what is it? And make it quick. It has been a long day."

"Yes, ma'am." Mrs. Saxon straightened herself up and backed up a few steps to face the entire council. Where they had ignored her before, they now all faced her since their supreme had given them permission. "My supreme, and members of the council. I believe we should not ignore our own history in the consideration of all actions we take. While it is the council's wish to continue this endeavor against the vampires, and you have your reasons. I must point out that we should not paint all vampires with the same broad brush as it appears you are. It would be important for each of us to remember why we each stay hidden from the rest of the world. At one time, they painted us with the broad brush and attempted to find and destroy anyone they could identify as a witch. Should we not be better than that and not repeat the same wrong that was inflicted on us?"

There were a few heads that nodded in the council, but not a single one spoke up in agreement. The perturbed look on the face of their supreme made sure of that. She let Mrs. Saxon stand there for a few seconds after she finished. The echo of her message, now just a distant memory in the rafters of the grand entry. Silence was its new occupant.

"Mrs. Saxon. The time and circumstances are different now, and–" Miss Roberts started, but Mrs. Wintercrest interrupted her objection with a wave of her hand. It both silenced her and annoyed her. A power I wish I had.

"Perhaps she has a point. One should never repeat their own history," suggested Mrs. Wintercrest. She turned and played to the other council members. They met her rather diplomatic statement with several smiles and nods of agreement, but still no one spoke. "We should consider our targets well. There is no need to-" What I saw next I would have never believed. Miss Roberts stepped forward and interrupted her own supreme. She reached forward, and with a hand on her shoulder, whispered something into her ear. From where I was, I could clearly see Mrs. Wintercrest's jaw twitch as Miss Roberts spoke to her, but I couldn't hear them, no matter how hard I tried.

Miss Roberts backed away, and Mrs. Wintercrest continued, "Mrs. Saxon, we thank you for your contribution, but I believe the times and circumstances are different, and frankly, it changes nothing. We are proceeding with efforts to hunt down and either eliminate or imprison all vampires for our own safety. You yourself should know how dangerous they are. You took in a young witch that was being hunted by a vampire." She then glanced back at her mini-me, in what I felt looked like a request for approval, which took me aback. What was this?

"Which you are giving refuge to, my supreme," interjected Mrs. Saxon.

Mrs. Saxon's observation caused a stir within the council, and Miss Roberts stepped forward. For what, I wasn't sure, but Mrs. Wintercrest blocked her, holding up her right hand, making sure we never found out. "Holding, until we can do a proper trial to determine his fate. We are more civilized than they are. Don't forget that. Rest assured, he will be dealt with."

"And what of the other vampires and rogue witches? Shouldn't they be afforded the opportunity of a trial?"

Mrs. Wintercrest received that suggestion like an offensive smell, distorting her appearance for a few seconds. Then I saw an expression that I had seen on her face too many times. Usually while I stood before her facing some odd accusation. That smug smile grew as she turned her head toward the council members. Miss Roberts leaned forward and whispered in her ear before she finally spoke. "Well, yes," she condescendingly agreed. "Those we capture will face a trial."

"Thank you, my supreme." Mrs. Saxon bowed slightly, and Mrs. Wintercrest turned to rejoin the rest of the council. "One last question, if it is permissible."

Mrs. Wintercrest stopped. She stood there for a few seconds before she turned around and acknowledged Mrs. Saxon. I couldn't see her face, but I knew she was stewing. I couldn't see the expression on Mrs. Saxon's face, either. Her back was to me, but I had a feeling she was standing there with her normal expression of quiet confidence, and enjoyed this little irritation. Something we both shared.

"Make it quick," Mrs. Wintercrest snapped.

"I believed this action by the council was targeted toward Jean and his followers, but in your discussion, I heard other areas mentioned. Did I hear incorrectly?"

"Mrs. Saxon. The council is taking up an effort to ensure our safety. That is all you need to know. This is a matter for the council, and none of your concern. Your presence was just a courtesy." Mrs. Wintercrest spun around on her heels and marched back to the front of the assembled council. The others turned forward as if to march out with her, but before she led them, she turned toward Mrs. Saxon once again. "I know what your concern is, and rest assured, if we run across your son, he will be granted certain considerations," she turned away.

"Assuming he doesn't take up arms against us," sniped Miss Roberts. She stood there and stared at Mrs. Saxon, almost as if she was hoping for a reaction from her.

I felt my body jerk at the statement. I wanted to jump up and do something, but I couldn't. All I could do was stay hidden and watch how Mrs. Saxon reacted. I was sure she had something more to say. I doubted she would plead or throw herself on the mercy of the council. Not that they had much mercy to give. I seriously doubted if Mrs. Wintercrest knew the meaning of the word. I was sure Miss Roberts didn't. I sat there waiting for Mrs. Saxon's response. This wasn't over. It couldn't be. I thought back to the few statements she had made. They were all carefully chosen points to make in front of the council. Each meant to plant thoughts and questions in their mind about what they were doing. She probably still had some hope that a member of the council would stand up and defy Mrs. Wintercrest. I didn't see a snowball's chance in hell of that, but Mrs. Saxon was more diplomatic than I was. Maybe that was why she said nothing. She just stood there and watched Mrs. Wintercrest lead the council down the hallway.

All the council members, aside from one, followed Mrs. Wintercrest into the hall almost in lockstep with one another. Miss Roberts stayed right where she was, in front of Mrs. Saxon. She appeared to be enjoying the moment. When the echo of the council's footsteps faded, she turned to follow them; striding with her head held high.

Mrs. Saxon waited until Miss Roberts disappeared down the hallway before she moved. I expected her to walk out the other way, but she turned and looked up right at me. I froze, not that I wasn't already frozen. How could she know I was here? It's not like she could hear me breathing.

I waited right where I was, still hidden behind the post, waiting for her to say something, but she didn't. She just kept her stare right up at me. Her expression was, well... blank. There was no frustration showing from her encounter with the council. None of the concerns I would have expected following Mrs. Wintercrest's last comment crept in. She turned and walked back down the hallway where she came from, leaving me with an icy feeling. Had she given up? She couldn't, could she? The Mrs. Saxon I knew wouldn't. I couldn't explain what I had just seen or felt.

I wasn't sure how much time had passed before I finally stood up and made my way to the door. I was still numb, and mostly moving on autopilot, thinking about what I had seen and what the expression on Mrs. Saxon's face meant. It couldn't mean what I thought it did. My legs moved me toward my room, while my brain considered other possibilities. None of them fit, which left me more dismayed than before. Maybe that was it. Maybe she had given up hope. It was a point I didn't want to accept, but it was all that remained. I paused at my door for the briefest of moments to wipe away a tear that had formed. I wasn't much of a crier, but it seemed over the last many months I had felt the sensation of the tear rolling down my cheek more than I had ever remembered before. I will say I was never in the emotional tempest I was in now, which had to be the principal contributor. I just didn't want Samantha to see me like this if she was awake. She was sleeping when I left.

"Holy Shit!" someone screamed behind me.

Crap! I've been busted!

13

My head collapsed forward, sending my forehead thudding against the door.

"Holy Shit!" she said again, this time her own hand muffled her voice. I heard another gasp from behind her. I turned my head and saw Apryl and Pamela in the hallway, shaking and bouncing.

"Where...? When did you get here?" Apryl asked. I stood up and hurried toward them, holding a finger up to my lips.

"Holy shit!" Apryl said again.

She wasn't going to be quiet, but I needed her to be. I took a more direct approach. I grabbed them both and rushed into Apryl's room, slamming the door behind us. Everyone on the floor was already used to Apryl slamming her door. This wouldn't draw any attention. Apryl bounced on the floor repeating what appeared to be her new favorite saying, and Pamela ran over to me and hugged me around the neck as I tried to explain.

"You two need to be quiet. Please!" I begged, keeping my voice in a hushed tone.

Apryl repeated her new favorite saying twice more before she stopped. Then it was her turn to hug me while I continued to beg.

"Please be quiet. No one is to know I am here."

Pamela stood back, grinning from ear to ear. Apryl let go of my neck, but as she backed up, her hands traced down my arms until she gripped my hands, pulling my arms out away from me a bit. She gave me a quick once over, and then looked at me cockeyed before she looked down again. "Seems you've lost weight."

I dropped her hands. "Look, a lot of stuff has been going on, but before I tell you anything. I need you to promise you won't tell a soul I'm here." I looked at Pamela, who agreed in an instant. Apryl was still looking for the baby bump that was no longer there. "Apryl?"

"This is different for you. Usually you are sneaking out, not in."

I let out an exacerbated sigh, a real one, and tilted my head and placed both hands on my hips. "Do you promise?"

"Yea. Yea. I promise," agreed Apryl, and it was a good thing too. I hadn't really considered what I would do if they hadn't. I guess I could have left with Samantha.

"I'm not sneaking back. I've been here for a little over a month."

"What?" This time it was Pamela who let the outburst slip, while Apryl bent over at the waist and then fell back on her bed.

"Where?" asked Apryl.

"In my room," I said, pointing across the hall to where my room was.

That sent Pamela into a stuttering fit as she backed up to the bed next to Apryl. "The whole time?" she asked once she pulled herself together.

"Yep," I nodded, and I figured I might as well tell them everything. "Mrs. Saxon rescued me and Marcus Meridian from Mordin and brought us back here. We've been in the room most of the time if you don't count a few trips out to the woods for training or Mrs. Tenderschott's classroom. Oh yeah, and the library."

Apryl's black eyes narrowed, and a sly grin crept across her face. "We?" she asked. "You and Marcus Meridian?"

I was shaking my head when Pamela asked, "What about Nathan?"

"No, it's not like that," and I sighed again. There was no way of getting around this now. "Marcus is somewhere only Mrs. Saxon knows. She won't even tell me." Come to think of it, I hadn't really asked. "I haven't seen Nathan since I went back to New Orleans to convince him to come home, and he said no."

"Wait. Wait." Apryl waved her arms in front of her. "You went back? When?"

"Right after Mrs. Saxon rescued me. I went back to bring him back, and because of..." I paused not really wanting to get into everything, but I couldn't see any way to avoid it, "... because of what the witches did, he no longer trusts us and stayed there with the other vampires."

"I can't really blame him," Apryl said. She winced as soon as the words left her mouth. "Sorry."

I let it go. I knew what she meant, and I couldn't really disagree, at least where the council was concerned.

"Wait!" Apryl pointed right at me and then hopped off the bed. "If *we've* been staying in your old room for about a month, and it's not that witch Marcus and it's not Nathan that means..." She cut off her own sentence with her hand, but the squeal that followed still made it through.

"Shush."

Apryl dropped her hand from her face and bounced on her feet, "I want to see. I want to see."

"See what?" Pamela asked, confused.

"Her baby," answered Apryl, with a slug to Pamela's arm.

"Baby?" she asked, still confused, and then I saw the light bulb click on behind her steadily growing smile. Her black eyes became as wide as the expanse of outer space.

"Wait! Wait! Wait!" I held up both hands to stop the rush toward the door. "Just wait!" I caught myself almost yelling and snapped my mouth shut. Both Apryl and

Pamela froze where they stood, and all three of us listened for the sound of anyone else moving in the hallway or one of the nearby rooms. There was nothing except the sound of the wind blowing outside. I lowered my hands and let out another involuntary breath. With it, I tried to release the tension I felt, and calmly said, "Just wait. Look, our presence here is supposed to be a secret. It's bad enough you already know that I am here. I can't."

"You don't trust us?" Apryl asked, and the question stung.

"It's not that. There is just a lot at risk here. My life. Her life, and really everybody else's too."

Apryl crossed her arms and scowled at me. "I forgot. You're Larissa Dubois. The woman that will save the world, all alone. I also forgot that you haven't needed any of our help along the way or ever trusted us." If her first accusation of not trusting them didn't sting, this one cut clear to the bone.

"No. It's not that," I said to apologize, but in truth, it kind of was. Mrs. Tenderschott had already told me of the interrogations of the other witches. Those witches that knew about me could handle that on their own, but a vampire would be helpless. "It's just.." I explained, but then that rationalization engine I called a brain kicked in and presented an argument that was hard to ignore. They already knew about me, and that also meant it exposed Samantha to the same risk whether or not they had seen her. So, I changed my answer. "There is something you need to know. She's not what you would expect." Now how to explain this? Words wouldn't really do it justice. At least not the ones I could put together. "Can you check to see if there is anyone in the hallway?"

I didn't have to ask twice. In an instant, Apryl ran out to the middle of the hallway. Once she surveyed it up and down, she motioned for us to follow. Just to be safe, I let Pamela go first. When she waved me in, I followed, and walked straight across to my room and opened the door. There was a chorus of silent giggling behind me, and I heard one of the two whispers of the word baby. I knew what they were expecting to find, and they would have if they had been here a month ago, a few hours after I gave birth.

The door opened, and they rushed in, stopping right inside the door. I had to give them a quick shove to make room for myself while I closed the door. Samantha was still asleep on her bed. I pushed through Apryl and Pamela and then walked over to her bed, where I sat and stroked her head. That was something I did often while holding her when she slept. It was a lot easier when she was smaller. I couldn't dare say younger because that was really just a week ago. That didn't mean I didn't still plan to hold her while she slept, no matter how big she had gotten. "Sam, can you wake up for a minute? I want you to meet two friends of mine."

She roused awake, and rolled over in my direction, opening her eyes. When she saw the two vampires standing there on the other side of the room, she sat up. It wasn't an abrupt or startled move, as most might make upon waking up to the sight of two vampires standing in your bedroom. But why would I expect her to react that way? She has seen that all her life. The abrupt and startled movements belonged to Apryl and Pamela, who appeared to struggle to understand what they saw.

"Apryl. Pamela. This is Samantha. My daughter." I let my brief introduction sink in for a moment. "I'm sure you both have some questions. Sam, this is Apryl, and Pamela. They are two of my closest friends."

"Mom?" Samantha asked curiously. "I thought we were supposed to be hidden."

The sound of her voice invoked another reaction from our two visitors.

"We are. Let's just say I messed up. I will explain later." I looked back at Apryl and Pamela. "Not what you were expecting?"

Both shook their heads and looked dumbfounded.

"Remember what Theodora told us about vampire pregnancies? It doesn't stop once they are born." I reached over and stroked my daughter's hair. I swear she had aged a few extra years since I left, and now looked only a year or two younger than myself. "Jen thinks she will hit an age and stop if she is a vampire. We just have to wait now."

Both of their jaws dropped to the floor, and I knew what that was from.

"Yes, she could be a vampire. We haven't tried anything to be sure, and before you both ask," I said with a finger up. "She is a witch. A very capable witch." I added with a great sense of pride, and I think Samantha felt that radiating from me. She, without any prompt from me, held open her hand as a whirlwind danced around on her palm before disappearing with a bright flash.

"So, she could be both, like you?" Pamela asked eagerly.

I nodded. "Could be. We just aren't sure." I replied, feeling odd talking about her like she wasn't in the room and yet she was sitting there in the bed next to me, while I still stroked her hair. So, I added my almost teenage daughter to the conversation. "Are we?" I asked, looking at her.

"Not yet. I don't crave blood, but I haven't really been around it. I eat normal food like everyone else here. I really love cheeseburgers, but mom," she stopped and stammered while she turned in the bed a little more toward me. "There are a few things I haven't told you yet. I have been experimenting on my own."

"You have?" I asked, sounding worried, but I was more concerned than worried. I hadn't seen Samantha look grim at all in her entire life, yet at this moment that was how she looked.

"I have. I was curious. I can hold my breath for a really long time."

"How long?" Apryl asked enthusiastically as she stepped forward in anticipation of the answer.

"About ten minutes, and I didn't even feel out of breath when I did it. I only let it out because I needed to answer one of Mrs. Tenderschott's questions."

"Interesting."

"Yes, it is," I said, agreeing with Apryl.

"She breathes, but can hold it that long. Could it be magic protecting her or something?"

Now that was a possibility I hadn't considered, and one I didn't even know if it was possible, but there was still so much I didn't know I couldn't dismiss it.

"She breathes?" asked Pamela.

"Yes, and she has a heartbeat." The heads of two of the three vampires in the room shot toward Samantha. They were searching for what they couldn't feel. Since Mrs. Saxon put up her block to protect us from anyone feeling her, she was a hole. A big null. A void. It was disconcerting. I knew it. I felt it when she first did it, but I got used to it. I needed to let them off the hook before they started doubting their own abilities. "Mrs. Saxon charmed the room to keep any of you from feeling it. Just to keep us hidden. I can't even feel it now either, but I did before that. Trust me, it's there, and it's strong."

Apryl stepped forward and held out her hand toward Samantha. "May I?" I knew she wanted to double check for herself, and I nodded, giving Samantha a reassuring pat on the shoulder.

Samantha held out her hand, and Apryl grabbed hold of it. Then she ran her other hand up Samantha's arm. She searched up and down her arm for the feeling of blood flowing under her skin. I knew it wasn't there, another sensation blocked by the charms, but that didn't stop Apryl from continuing to search.

"Odd. It's not there, but something else is. She is warm to the touch, but my icy touch doesn't cause any goose pimples."

"It doesn't?" I yanked Samantha's arm from Apryl to check for myself. I might have done it a little too hard. "I'm so sorry. Are you okay?" I reached over and hugged her.

"Yes mom. I'm fine. It didn't hurt."

"It didn't?" I asked again, just to be sure, as I released her.

"No." She shook her head and twisted her arm back and forth to show me it was fine. I took her arm in my hand, gentler this time, and rubbed my hand up and down it. She shivered, but Apryl was right. Her skin never changed. Odd. I looked up at Apryl, amazed. Nathan's skin always went gooseflesh when I touched him. Maybe she had gotten used to it.

"I think we need to set up some vampire trials to find out."

"What are vampire trials? Are they like the seven wonders?"

Apryl burst out laughing at Samantha's questions, and I knew why. There was no such thing as vampire trials, at least nothing as formal as the seven wonders. I didn't have any idea what Apryl had in mind, but she was right on the thought. We needed to find out for sure.

14

During the night, I filled them in on everything I knew. There didn't seem to be any reason not to anymore. I was the big secret, and they already knew about that. Everything else they either knew part of or had heard rumors of going around the coven. They also brought me up on what was happening in the coven. I played dump as Apryl recounted how Gwen tortured her with the charm. To hear her tell it, the charm brought her close to death. I could see that if you were exposed long enough, and I had no doubt that Gwen prolonged it as much as she could. There were more stories they shared, some where my name was basically burned in effigy. Not all that shocking considering my standing with the council. Hearing Gwen's name in each story wasn't that shocking either. It seemed with the council here; Gwen had become more of a little "witch" than I remembered.

We did our best to keep things down to not wake Samantha up. She didn't share the same gift, or curse, we did. At least not to the level of not having to sleep. She still needed that every night, and the few nights she didn't sleep well, she was a bit of a grouch in the morning. A morning person my daughter was not. That gave us plenty of time to talk about what Apryl called the "vampire trials". We needed to find out if there was any part of her was vampire. I rejected Apryl's first suggestion. There was no way I was going to take my daughter out on a hunt to let her feed and see how she reacts. No way. No how. There had to be other ways.

Pamela, who also shook her head at Apryl's suggestion, came up with another plan which focused more on the physical attributes. Our speed, endurance, and strength. It seemed like a good approach that would absolutely do it. She just needed to promise not to use magic to improve her skills. When to do the test was yet to be decided, but where was clear. We would need to sneak out again, but I didn't think that was a problem any longer.

When they left to get ready for their classes, we did the same. It wouldn't be long before Master Thomas popped in for our morning session. My first therapy session of the day with Edward would follow that. Samantha would receive her private lessons with Master Thomas while I answered the same questions I did yesterday for Edward. I wasn't sure if he expected different answers every day or not. He knew the cause now, and he also knew what it took to fix it, even though he didn't want to accept it. This was our routine day after day, and it had a pleasant rhythm to it, which, believe it or not, had a calming effect on both of us. Samantha always appeared calm. She was the typical happy-go-lucky child that enjoyed learning all she could do in the magical world around her, unless her mother did something stupid and she needed to bail her out. For me, it filled the time and kept me from circling that void. That didn't mean some of my gloominess didn't rub off on her.

I often caught myself sitting and looking out the window, missing Nathan with every fiber of my being. I wasn't just hurting for me. I was hurting for Samantha too. She was missing all these moments with her father, and he was missing everything with his daughter. Her first words, her first steps, and not to mention her first spell. That broke my heart more than not feeling his arms around me. Things became gloomier after I heard his voice call out to me yesterday, and then again last night. It wasn't a longing or a missing that I felt. Those would feel like happy emotions compared to this. This was a loss and fear, and they physically drained me. It was no longer a wonder of where he was. It was an obsession. I even stared out the window, as if I could see him if I tried hard enough. When I didn't, I fell further into my personal pit of despair, and just like she had many times before, Samantha sensed it, and came over and wrapped her arms around me. Now they could wrap all the way around me, seeing that she was almost as tall as I was. She always asked me what was wrong, and I always told her the same. "Nothing. Just thinking."

We never really talked about her father. I mean, she knows she has one, and she knows he isn't here with us, and when the topic of him comes up, I say he will be with us soon and that is it. I haven't gone into the love story of Larissa and Nathan, the classic Greek tragedy. Perhaps either of us could be the tragic hero in that story. One day she will know everything, but not until he is here with us, and she can get to know him and hear it from both of us.

Right on schedule, Master Thomas appeared, and our day began. Samantha greeted Master Thomas with a hug.

"Morning Samantha, Larissa."

"Morning Master Thomas," Samantha greeted him cheerily. I said nothing, and just climbed off the windowsill I was perched on, and readied myself for our training, or what I saw was an exercise in futility. I hated to break it to Master Thomas. His theory that magic is like a muscle wasn't exactly working here. My magic was all tangled up in the world's biggest charley horse and no amount of work had even loosened it a bit. Only the rancid contents of those jars had.

"It looks like rain outside, so we are going somewhere else this morning. Shall we?" He didn't wait for an answer. He never did. With a quick spin of his arm, a portal opened, and he and Samantha hurried through. I started for the portal and then stopped, knowing I needed to drink a jar first. I walked over to them with the portal still spinning behind me, waiting for me. My hand hovered over the jars. Not because of the horrible tasting concoction they held, but because I knew I needed to preserve them for what I had planned. There were only three left, and I needed one for my training today. I saw this problem as an equation that would not work out in my favor, and it wasn't because I hated math. I knew a little sip would not cut it. That was a fact I found out the hard way last night. Maybe I could get away with half, saving some for another day. How long would that half last me? We were about to find out.

I drank that half and followed them blindly through the portal, emerging into a room that was all too familiar. One that had been used for secret classes before, and seemed fitting to be used for that again. The moment my foot hit the stone floor and I saw my first large stone archway, I knew exactly where I was. I was back at the scene of the crime. The place where Master Thomas had laid his master plan on me. Our secret plan, which, as it turns out, wasn't all that secret.

"Larissa, it's so good to see you." Mr. Demius, our master of the dark arts, approached me and warmly hugged me. Then he turned and hugged my daughter just as warmly. "So, have you been practicing?"

"Yes, I have," responded Samantha.

"You've been teaching her?" I asked curiously. It seemed someone else had been getting some secret training of her own.

"Of course," he said, with a look of shock that I didn't know. "We all have while you are going through your training and other sessions. She is a fast learner, just like her mother." He looked at her and did something I hadn't seen often. He smiled.

I stood there and waited for that little girl giggle I had heard from her for a few days when someone complimented her. Maybe it was her nervous laugh when she received attention. I used to do the same when I was younger. Usually when my parents were bragging about me. This time, it never arrived, and I looked to see a pleasant and confident look on my daughter's face. She was growing up, more than just in her height. How was it possible for someone to grow and mature years in just a month? I didn't know. Just another one of the mysteries of the universe that I didn't have answers to. Add it to the rather long list I had accumulated.

"Let's get started," Master Thomas barked.

"Training calls." I waved bye to Mr. Demius, but I watched over my shoulder as he and Samantha headed down to the front of his classroom for her own training. I had to admit, I was a little distracted as Master Thomas put me through the paces.

It was the same every day. Our routine was like morning calisthenics, if you subscribe to his theory that magic was like a muscle.. It was the same thing every day. We started with simple telekinesis, my specialty, and then moved on to creating fire and other elemental magic. We usually stopped with some fire tricks and maybe a little air movement, which, to be honest, I never really enjoyed before. It seemed boring to me compared to sending a huge fireball racing across the room, but just being able to do something like that in my current situation felt good.

My distracted state showed up when he asked me to try one more elemental trick by controlling water. This was something he and Master Demius had me perform before in this class. It was a three-part request. First, I had to create some in the basin against the wall. Then, I had to pull it from the basin toward me while in complete control of it, causing it to change shape and direction. The last step was one that took a lot of practice before, but again one that once I mastered it seemed impressive. Right there in the classroom, I needed to produce a small thunderstorm, by turning the water into a cloud and then compressing it harder and harder. I wasn't sure if Master Thomas intended for me do that last step today. It didn't matter; I didn't get that far. I lost a little control, make that a lot of control, while I was calling it to me, and the water fell to Mr. Demius's floor with a splash. In my defense, it wasn't exactly my fault. How could I focus on what I was doing when my daughter was learning her first rune from Mr. Demius on the other side of the room? I heard them talking about it, and he was giving her the same descriptions and instructions my mother gave me. It was hard enough not to stop all together and watch as she created a floor of grass under her feet. Too bad the water I dropped wasn't closer to them and I couldn't make the excuse I was trying to water it.

"You need to stay focused," cautioned Master Thomas, while Mr. Demius scowled at the puddle on his floor before he waved a hand, sending it back to the basin. "Push all those concerns and thoughts you have out of the way. They are controlling you."

He was clueless at what this distraction was until he finally caught where my eyes were looking, and then he turned and stood next to me, sharing the same view. "She is quite amazing, isn't she? Watching her learn and negotiate her way through spells and other witchcraft, you would think she has been doing this all her life." He caught himself, and we shared a look. "Okay, I walked into that one, but you know what I mean. She has only been at this a few weeks and is still more capable than most of those studying here in this coven."

Mr. Demius continued to drill her on creation by having her form everything from living plants to inanimate objects like chairs, rocks, and tables. I knew what he had her created wasn't as important as her learning exactly how she created such a variety of objects. Once she understood that, she could create anything. I couldn't be prouder. I only wished Nathan was here to see the young woman she had become.

"I think it's because of her family," he said with a wink. "Your family is a powerful family, and add in Mrs. Saxon's contribution. That combination couldn't produce anything but..."

"I thought it could skip a generation?" I interrupted his compliment. He was right, and it caused the pride to well up inside of me, but there was a fact to consider in there. It had skipped Nathan.

"Well, yes," he stammered. "It can skip a few generations," he continued, still stammering. "Take Nathan, for example. It obviously skipped him, but that doesn't take away from his family." He walked forward toward my daughter and Mr. Demius. "Demius, let me have a go," he offered, and at that moment, I knew my training was done for the day.

It was both a relief and a disappointment. I was tired of the same old frustrating attempts that resulted in nothing more than a few birthday party magician tricks. Okay, maybe I was being a little overdramatic and giving birthday part magicians too much credit, but it wasn't what I was used to, and wasn't want I needed. As I watched Mr. Demius let Master Thomas take his place in the training my daughter, I had to wonder; maybe I wasn't the answer after all. Maybe it was Samantha. No! I shook that thought from my head. I wouldn't put that pressure on her. This was my job, and I needed to handle things myself, so I did the only thing I could do. I started practicing by myself.

"Still not focused?" asked Mr. Demius as he approached. I dropped my hands before I attempted my first spell on my own. I hadn't even decided what to try first.

"That's always my problem," I said, with a hint of venom. That word was one he had practically beaten into my head during our original refresher sessions.

"No. It's different this time."

I raised my hands and started again. Where would I start? I guess where I left off. Back to the elemental magic, skipping water for obvious reasons. Wind it would be. I picked a corner of the room and held out my hands as if to guide the air around in a swirl, but Mr. Demius grabbed them and placed them down by my side.

"Why don't you rest and relax for a minute? I know what Master Thomas is trying to do, but all it's going to do is compound your frustration as you struggle with things you know inside you should be able to do easily."

Finally, someone that spoke common sense around here.

He stood beside me, watching the lesson on the other side of the room. "Remember what I once said. Stronger focus makes stronger magic. The more frustrated you become, the less control you will have."

"Tell me something I don't know."

He laughed, which was the first time I had ever heard it. It was a jolly one at that. Our dark arts master. The king of everything that scared most people had a jolly laugh. "You would be the expert on that subject. From the day I met you, you have always had something clouding your mind."

Wait? Was that a shot at me? "I guess I'm complicated then," I sniped back rather shortly.

"Not at all. You have powerful emotions, and before you take that the wrong way," he warned, and it was a good thing he did. He was about to find out how strong my emotions were and how well they were dealing with everything at the moment. Mount Saint Helens would seem popgun compared to what was about to erupt, and this would be all me, no magic at all. "That is what makes you a powerful witch. Oh, sure, anyone born into a family of witches can perform magic. Plenty of examples of that have come through this coven. There are several of them here now, but how great you are depends on how much you care, how strongly you feel, and how well you can focus that." His eyes cut in my direction. "Tiring of that word, aren't you?"

"No, because it's true," I replied calmly, believing that the answer would earn me some points and make me seem mature.

"Oh, come on," he chided. "I saw the grimace on your face. We have basically beat it into you with a bat since you got here. It's only because we all know how great you could be if you can just harness it. Focusing and clearing your mind doesn't mean being void of emotions. It means controlling them. Removing the feeling of chaos and feeling the power of those emotions flowing through you. Look at your daughter over there. She is full of joy, and it shows in how easy she is performing. You right now, you're a mess, and it is completely understandable with everything you have gone through. Beating yourself up about your struggles with magic won't solve this. Give yourself a break."

"I've done everything but physically beat myself up, and nothing's worked," I huffed.

Then it happened again. Another uncharacteristic moment as Mr. Demius put a supportive arm around my shoulders. "The problem is you are doing all the wrong things. You and I both know what you must do, and there isn't anything else you can do that will fix this. There is no potion. There is no spell. There is no secret to force the magic out. It's bottled up in you with all your emotions and uncertainty, and there is only one way to unleash it."

I stood there in shock. Were he and I in agreement on this? Was that even possible? Or was this another ruse, like my secret training before, that wasn't all that secret? That had to be it, and I would not be the pawn in this game anymore and I called him on it. "Let me guess. This is all part of some plan concocted by Mrs. Saxon to tell me to do what I know I should, without her really being involved, like my supposedly secret training?"

He just shook his head. "No Larissa. This is just you and I talking. She knows what you need to do, and we have talked about it, but she is concerned that you entering the chaos that is going on will just unsettle things even more. Further hindering your chances of fulfilling what we all hope you can become." His head bounced back and forth as if he were considering two sides of an argument. Then, with a skewed smile, "She might be right, but I think interjecting a little instability into this chaos might just be what is needed. Not to mention, if you don't, this problem will never solve itself, now will it?"

He had a point that I agreed to with silence. "Does he know?" I nodded toward Master Thomas.

"He knows what you need, but he agrees with Mrs. Saxon. They are both of the camp that either Nathan will find his way here, or in time, your emotions will fade and settle all on your own. But we both know how strong that bond you feel is, especially now that you share a daughter. That won't happen anytime soon, if ever."

"But" I said rather loudly, causing a look from both Samantha and Master Thomas. I let the silence in the room settle back around us, and for them to resume their lesson before I asked what burned at the tip of my tongue. "Mrs. Saxon. Shouldn't she already know? She seems to know everything else that is going to happen."

"You mean her divination?"

"Yes. She said she saw me coming and knew how my path would lead."

"Which she may," Mr. Demius said, "I know her well enough to know how much she loves and cherishes her son. If she had any visions about what would happen to him, where he was, and when he would come back, she wouldn't be standing around. A mother's love is the strongest bond in the world. After she lost her husband, Nathan became her world. If I had to guess based on how she has been working the council, and all the questions I overhear her ask Jen and Kevin, she doesn't see his future all that clearly at the moment. If she sees it at all."

"So, it's up to me?"

"I'm afraid so."

Even after the conversation we just had, hearing his very frank answer was a shock. He was practically telling me to do everything that everyone else here was telling me not to. I was so stunned; and speechless, which was an odd state for me to find myself in. I just stood there and watched my daughter and Master Thomas work across the way, while I thought over what Mr. Demius had told me. It was what I already knew, but to hear someone else say it added more fuel to what was already burning inside.

"Larissa," he said, his voice steady and reassuring, "set aside your concerns for others. Trust your instincts and do what you believe is right. Mrs. Saxon's opinion, Benjamin's thoughts—let them fade away. If deep inside, you know it's the path to follow, then it is." He turned and gripped me by the shoulders and locked his eyes with mine. "And most importantly, disregard the council's judgment. Some may react with outrage, but once you fulfill your destiny, the rest will rally behind you. Trust me on that."

"Don't worry. I don't give a rat's ass what they think."

"Good," Mr. Demius commented while releasing me.

"Plus, there seems to be something going on there anyway," I remarked. It was just an off-the-cuff remark, but it got Mr. Demius's full attention.

"So, you have noticed it too?"

"Miss Roberts?" I asked.

"Mmm hmm," he responded. "It has been that way for several years now."

Master Thomas finished his lesson with Samantha before Mr. Demius could elaborate. As they walked toward us, Master Thomas gave her one final pointer. If I had to bet, it was probably something about focus. It was his favorite. I had heard it more times than I wanted to remember. That gave me another moment alone with Mr. Demius, and considering the conversation we had just had, I saw an opening.

"Mr. Demius. I was reading through an old book of spells Edward found for me," no lie there, "and I came across a related spell I didn't know. Congero. Do you know what that is?"

"I do. You really should study your Latin more. Congero. To amass or accumulate. It's a potion, not a spell. You can use it to increase the volume of a substance. The Italians mostly used it to make more wine." His right hand found his chin and stroked it. "Come to think of it, that is really the only use I have seen, but never mind," he gathered himself. "It's an old spell, but it works."

I waited for him to ask why I wanted to know, and what spell I was looking up that referenced that, but he never did. He just let the answer sit there until Samantha and Master Thomas finished the discussion they were having about his last piece of advice, which I was still assuming was about focus until I heard otherwise.

"Truly amazing Samantha. Truly amazing."

My daughter beamed from ear to ear at Mr. Demius's compliment. I had to admit I was beaming, too. He was one hundred percent correct. She was amazing in so many ways, most of which had nothing to do with what she and Master Thomas were just working on. She was a witch, and an amazing one at that, but she was so much more.

"This was a great session. Both of you," Master Thomas looked us both in the eye. "Students will be coming in soon, so you need to head back up to your room." He spun open a portal back to my room while he said, "I will be back up this afternoon for your second session. Don't forget your session with Edward around noon."

How could I forget? I thought as I put my arm around my daughter and started for the portal. I saw a figure waiting for us and gave Samantha a little shove forward. and turned to Master Thomas and Mr. Demius. "Master Thomas, what time is our afternoon session?" I asked as I walked backward toward the portal, doing my best to hold their attention. I knew good and well the session was at five this afternoon, just like it always was.

"Five," he answered curiously.

"Oh, that's right," I remarked, as my back foot stepped through. "See you then." I stepped through. The portal closed right in my face.

"That was close," Lisa said with a long exhale. Samantha ran over to Lisa and gave her a big hug. "I was just standing here, and the portal opened right in front of me."

"We're lucky they didn't see you. What are you doing here?

"Mission accomplished," she said, pulling a piece of paper out of her pocket. "I know what Congero is and why it is important."

"Me too."

15

"We can use Congero to stretch a single drop of blood into all the blood we need," Lisa enthusiastically proclaimed.

"Absolutely. Why didn't I make the connection?" I wondered aloud.

Lisa and I were absolutely ecstatic! We were practically jumping out of our skins with excitement as we celebrated our discovery! This was the last piece of the puzzle. Now I just needed to put it all together and hope it worked.

"And there are only three ingredients. I know exactly where they are in Mrs. Tenderschott's classroom," continued Lisa.

My enthusiasm about my own discovery took a bit of a downturn. She had made it further than I had. I hadn't thought to ask Mr. Demius about the ingredients or how to do it. The thrill of knowing what the spell was had probably blinded me from all I didn't know, but needed to know about it. Thank God Lisa had thought about that and asked. If I went back to Mr. Demius now, he might ask what I was using it for. Though I don't believe he would attempt to stop me after our little discussion. He might even help. That was a thought. Having someone with his experience would be a boost, especially with me in my current state. But I dismissed that before I let the thought gain any more momentum. I couldn't put anyone else at risk. Too many have paid a price because of me.

"I can grab them tonight and bring them back up." Lisa leaned in and added, "I just learned a little invisibility spell. I have been dying to try."

"Invisibility?" I asked, thinking about all the uses I could have for something like that in my present status of confinement. "Does it make you fully invisible?"

"Yep. They can't see or hear..." Lisa stopped. Her enthusiasm drained away, and she looked past me, over my shoulder, with deep concern. I turned and saw a similar expression looking back at us.

"Samantha, what's wrong?"

"Oh nothing," she said. "Just listening in on some weird vampire plan. Lisa, I thought you were just a witch, not both, like my mother."

"I am just a witch. Why?" Then a big toothy grin appeared on Lisa's face, and it appeared she answered her own question. "I get it. The plan to create a lot of blooood." Lisa exaggerated the last word and threw in her best Count Dracula impersonation on top of it.

Oh, lord. She didn't have a clue what we were talking about. To her, it probably sounded as if we were planning a banquet for vampires. I guess we needed to explain our little plan to Samantha, especially since she is a major player, or piece of it.

"Samantha, it's not what it sounds like."

"Oh, it's exactly what it sounded like," giggled Lisa.

"Stop it." I slapped her on the shoulder. "The blood is not for what you think it is. It has nothing to do with vampires, and actually," I straightened up after thinking of this point and channeled my inner Mrs. Saxon. "It has everything to do with being a witch. Why don't you have a seat on your bed, and I will explain everything to you."

Samantha still looked concerned, but walked back and sat on the edge of her bed with only a slight hesitation.

"Where to start?"

"Why not start with your problem? It might help for her to understand the why."

"Yes," I agreed. Lisa was absolutely right. It was an obvious place. Understanding the why would help her understand the necessity for what we were going to do, and not to mention it would finally address the elephant in the room. Her father. It's not that she or I ever tap danced around the topic. We just hadn't discussed *everything*, and in this case, *everything* was really *everything*.

"Sam, you know how mom is having trouble with her magic?"

She nodded, then looked at the tray of jars. Two of which were still full, and another sat next to those, half full. "It's why you have to drink those before any training."

"That's right, but I'm not sure you understand why I am having problems."

"Mom. I might be young, but I'm not stupid. You miss my father, and that has you all confused and out of focus."

From the mouth of babes. She nailed it. She completely nailed it and said it better than anyone else had. Even me, but if only it were that simple.

"I've heard you talking to others, and it makes complete sense. So, you need to find him and bring him home."

Dang. I almost had to reach up with a hand to make sure my jaw hadn't dropped. My almost a month and a half old daughter, that now looked like she was going on fifteen, understood it all, or let's make that most of it. There were some details missing. Ones she would have had no way of knowing. I never discussed them in front of her.

"That's right." I swallowed hard to push down the nerves that were bubbling up inside. "But there is more to the story." I paused, worried what I felt welling up inside would cause me to break down. I took a few beats to gather myself. I looked down and locked my eyes with Samantha's. That was when I realized what I felt wasn't so much a worry about me breaking down while I told her. It was the concern that what I was about to tell her would destroy her. "Your father is Nathan Saxon."

Her eyes jerked, causing me to stop. "Mrs. Saxon is my grandmother?"

"Yes," I said, with a sigh, feeling even more guilty than I had ever imagined I would have about withholding that little detail. It was bad enough she was missing the opportunity to get to know her father, but I had also denied her from knowing who her grandmother was. Yes, she was still a part of her life, but who she was to Samantha was a secret that I had kept, until now. A secret that Ms. Saxon agreed with.

"She never said anything. I just thought she was just being nice."

"No Sam, she is your grandmother."

"Why didn't you tell me?" Samantha's eyes searched me for answers. Those answers led down a path that I didn't want to go down, but I had to. "I wanted you to get to know your father by actually getting to know your father, and not by what you might hear from me, Mrs. Saxon, or anyone else. Does that make sense?"

"I guess, but…" she started and then bit her lip and looked up at me.

"Go on Sam, but what?"

"Why couldn't I know who he is?"

I swallowed hard. I knew what I had to say. Just saying the words would tear me to pieces, but that was nothing compared to what I feared it would do to her. Whatever family image she had in her head was about to be shattered. "I'm afraid some of it is bad news." My warning appeared to have snuffed out that light. "Yes Nathan, her son, is your father."

Oh God, how do I do this? I tried to convince myself she had to know. She had to know everything, but it was something about looking into her deep green eyes that made me reconsider leaving out details. I could tell her without telling her all the horrifying pieces. But to what end? She would eventually find out, and the time needed to be now. "He was a mortal when we met," I choked out. "Which means he wasn't a witch or a vampire. A few weeks before you were born, a vampire named Jean St. Claire attacked us, and Nathan saved my life, but he was bit and became a vampire." A quiver developed in Samantha's bottom lip. I hadn't even made it to the worst of it yet.

"Now this might be hard to understand. I actually don't understand it all yet. The Council of Mages attacked us while we were in New Orleans, separating us. I have tried to find him, but the council has continued to attack them, turning him against anything to do with witches. He is lost and confused and needs us to help bring him home. Understand?"

"Why are they attacking?" Samantha asked. Every word shook as her voice cracked multiple times.

"I don't know, to be honest. I have a theory, but I don't know if I am right, and that isn't really that important. What is important is finding Nathan and bringing him back home, where he can be safe with us."

Samantha nodded, quivering chin and all. I walked over and sat next to her and took her hand in mine. It trembled.

"Now, there is a spell that will help us find him, but I am going to need your help with it."

"Okay, just show me what I need to do." Samantha wiped away a rogue tear and looked at me eagerly. She still looked devastated, but I knew what she was feeling. The hope of a resolution. The hope of ending the hurt. Even if that hurt may have just started.

"We need a drop of your blood."

She lurched back away from me, and I felt her hand jerk, but she didn't jerk it completely out of my hand. "My blood?"

"Yes, you are his daughter, and this spell needs the blood of a direct relative. The closer the relation, the better." I searched her face for understanding and found just a hint.

"So, you don't need me to help with performing the spell?"

"Oh, I will need someone's help with that, for sure, but first we need a drop of your blood. Then we will use a potion, Congero. The one you heard Lisa and I talking about. We need to use that to create enough blood to cover a large piece of parchment. According to what I read, if we do this right, it will draw a map to him on the parchment."

"Okay, let me get this right," Samantha asked, peering at me and then Lisa. "You need to use a potion to create enough of my blood to spread across a large piece of paper so another spell can draw a map on it that will lead to my father?"

"Pretty much," I nodded, and then to help reinforce it a little more I sprung up off the bed, almost forgetting to let go of her hand first, and then sprinted across the room to the desk, where I grabbed the book that was still open to that page. I sat back down and placed the book on her lap and turned it back one page to the start of the spell. When I pointed at the top, Samantha started reading on her own. Her eyes grew in size the further she read. When she finally reached the end, she looked up, but said nothing.

"See, it's all there," I said, picking the book up and setting it down beside me, careful not to lose the page.

"Okay." Samantha let out a long and slow exhale, and cautiously asked, "How do we do this?"

"We need some ingredients," I said and looked right at Lisa, then I made my way to my desk. "You have the list for Congero, and here is the list for the rest of the spell." I grabbed a pencil and paper and scribbled the list quickly, before I handed the paper to Lisa.

16

Operation Blood-Map was in full go when the clock rolled over to nine that night. That was the name Apryl gave it when I told her about the plan. Right on time, a portal opened, and Lisa stepped through, wearing a plaid backpack over the top of a long black coat. When I saw Jack following her, I walked forward with my hands outstretched to block him.

"No. No. No. Not going to happen."

The portal closed before I could send him back through. I had already spent the better part of the last hour trying to tell Apryl she wasn't coming with me. This wasn't even a case where I had to convince her. The answer was a flat no. No one was. Just me. This was something I had to do, and I would not risk anyone else. Apryl kept arguing and even challenged me to stop her, which would be easier than she might believe. The others might be a problem. Once they knew where I was going, they could easily pop in there on their own.

"Jack needs to go back now!"

"I need some help to carry everything, and you are going to need some help. Those jars won't last you that long."

Based on my best guess, they were going to last maybe a day, but I didn't plan on using them unless I needed them. I was going there purely as a vampire, and I would have to rely on my speed and strength to find Nathan. In the plan I had worked out in my head, I would drink the half full one before I left so I could open a portal and have a little with me, but after that, I wouldn't touch it unless it was an emergency, or we were ready to come home. That was it.

"I can't ask you, and I won't let you. This is too dangerous on so many levels." Rogue witches were running around, attacking anything they believe was related to the council. Vampires were attacking anything they believed was a witch. The council's warriors were attacking both. I was walking into a war zone. The benefit I had over the others, I couldn't easily die. Not like Lisa or Jack could.

"You can't really stop us," Jack said forcefully as he stepped forward, as if some hero in a war movie stepping across a line drawn on the ground. The difference was, there wasn't a line, and I wasn't asking for volunteers.

"I can, and I will." I was bluffing, because I knew I couldn't, but I sure hoped he hadn't figured that out yet.

"This isn't Larissa against the world," he said firmly, staring right into my black eyes. I watched his expression and his chin never flinched. For a fleeting moment, I felt something for him I hadn't before. I actually had a brother. Wow, how far we had come.

"We can discuss that later." Lisa stepped between us. "I still need his help to gather the ingredients, and the last time we checked, your magic isn't that reliable. Seeing that he is the only other witch around here that knows you are even here, he was the only choice."

I looked at both of them. Their hands were empty, and Lisa's backpack hung limp from her shoulder. That meant they hadn't gathered them yet. "Where are they?"

"Still in Mrs. Tenderschott's classroom," Lisa said, and then held up a cautionary finger.

"And why? We kind of need them here." Her finger would not stop me from asking the obvious question.

"We do, but we need help."

She had already explained that as the reason she brought Jack. That was why my next move was to thrust my hand toward Jack and shake it to say—he's right there.

"No. He will help carry things, but even though Mrs. Tenderschott won't be able to see or hear us, she may notice things disappearing off her shelves. I've already popped down there twice, and she is still mulling around her classroom. It seems they have canceled the nightly tea they usually have with the council."

Tea? All sorts of odd images rolled in my head of that eclectic group sitting around with our instructions, pinkies extended while they drank tea and talked. They canceled it. I wondered if Mrs. Saxon's protest had something to do with that?

"We need either you or Sam to distract her while Jack and I do some shopping."

Okay, I saw where this was going, and I was all ready to volunteer, but someone beat me to it.

"I'll do it." Samantha leaped up from the bed and practically hopped across the floor at the opportunity.

"We both will. The two of us will be a better distraction than just one." I would not bow out that easily, plus as I saw it. One of us would need to keep a watch for where the activity was happening, so we could divert her away.

"Good then. When you're ready, head on down. We will pop down a few minutes after you."

Well, there was no time like the present. I looked at Samantha and motioned after her. Then I pointed right at Apryl. "You need to be gone by the time we get back."

Samantha immediately opened a portal and stepped through first. Then she motioned for me before saying, loud enough for everyone to hear. "It's all clear mom."

That was my cue, and I followed her through.

"Well, isn't this a pleasant surprise," cooed Mrs. Tenderschott from the front of the room. She was slaving over a stack of papers.

"I hope we aren't interrupting. We were bored and thought we'd come visit our favorite person."

"Not at all. I'm grading some tests," she explained while flipping through the stack. "I bet you don't miss this."

"I sure don't," I agreed as we walked to the front of the room and took our usual spots across the table from her.

"So, what's new with you two? Any break throughs?" she asked, directing the question at me.

"Not yet," I said with a reserved sigh. I didn't want to oversell our act, but as much as I tried not to, I caught myself being more deliberate with my speech and more animated with my arms and hands with every word. I told myself to relax. Mrs. Tenderschott wouldn't guess what we were doing in a thousand years. We had nothing to be worried about. I just needed to act naturally. Which was all fine to say, but doing it was something altogether different. I felt my body tense up, as a jar on the shelf behind her lifted and disappeared.

"I had hoped by now something would have worked. Are you still working with Master Thomas?"

"Yes. Twice a day, and sometimes Mrs. Saxon is there too. Sam is working with Master Thomas as well and is becoming quite good." I said to shift the attention away from myself. My nerves were getting to me. I wasn't sure if it was because I was deceiving her, or the worry I felt when it appeared someone almost dropped a jar behind her. They may be invisible, but graceful, they were not.

"Oh, I know. I have heard," she said, and turned her attention to Samantha. "They both brag about you often. Sam, I am curious. Does it come easy to you, or are you having to put a lot of concentration into it?"

Samantha didn't answer immediately. The floating objects behind Mrs. Tenderschott distracted her. Jar after jar lifted before being replaced back in their initial resting place. Lisa may have known where all the ingredients were, but I am guessing Jack didn't have a clue and was having to search jar by jar.

"Sam?" I whispered, to prompt her, but again she didn't answer, and now Mrs. Tenderschott turned around to follow her gaze. My hand slapped against my face, and I tried to hide my eyes and face. We had just been caught. But like with most things in the world, timing is everything. When Mrs. Tenderschott turned around, nothing was out of place or floating. It was as if they were not even there. I avoided letting out a stress filled exhale.

I elbowed Samantha, and she jerked out of her trance and answered Mrs. Tenderschott's question. "Yes ma'am. Most things have been pretty easy."

"That's a great sign. Your mother struggled at first," Mrs. Tenderschott said with a wink.

"That's not entirely true," I protested as two beakers of something brown were taken off the shelf to her left.

"Didn't you set your dresser on fire? And didn't you also burn down Mr. Helms' classroom?"

"Mom?" Samantha squealed. "Did you?"

"Yes, but…" I held up a hand to stop any interruptions before I corrected the facts here. "That was not my first attempts. I was like you and able to learn new abilities quickly when I was first learning. The second time around, I was a little out of practice. It had been close to eighty years. Hell, I didn't even know I was a witch."

"That didn't stop you from sending Jack across the pool." Mrs. Tenderschott grinned wildly. A jar jostled slightly. All three of us turned in the sound's direction, but none of us saw anything. "Probably just a top I didn't put on tightly settling," Mrs. Tenderschott uttered, and got up.

"Mom, you threw Jack across the pool?" asked Samantha, taking her turn to bail us all out.

"He made me mad."

"Well, I will admit, back then he had a way of doing that to everyone," agreed Mrs. Tenderschott. She settled back down on her stool. "Samantha, that was how we found out your mother was a witch. See, when she arrived, we just thought she was a vampire. We knew there was a mystery about her, but we didn't know that the mystery was both who and what she was. Then one day Jack made some comment to her out at the pool."

"He called me an orphan," I interjected.

"Ah, so that is what he said. Now that I know what it was, I can agree. He got what he deserved. Your mom used telekinesis to throw him across the pool. I'm sure others wish they could have done the same. Jack had a way of rubbing people the wrong way."

"He's grown on me." I added, and just cringed, waiting to hear the clang of another jar, but there was only silence.

For the next forty minutes, Mrs. Tenderschott dragged me down memory lane in front of my daughter. Some of them were embarrassing stories, but others were some of my finer moments. A few I didn't really remember as grandly as she did. I think she embellished a bit, but I didn't mind. Especially when they were stories about me getting the better of Gwen. I quite enjoyed them.

It had been a while since I had seen anything move or disappear in the classroom. I hoped that meant they were done and gone, but there was no way to be sure. I glanced around the room again and saw nothing moving. What they were after shouldn't have taken that long to gather up. Of course, first they had to find it, and she had hundreds upon hundreds of jars and boxes of things on those shelves. Just to be sure, I took another glance around, and again saw nothing. I also listened for the beating of their hearts and took in a sniff for that metallic richness that flowed through their veins. Either they were gone, or that invisibility spell Lisa used covered everything. We took her next pause between stories as an opportunity to return to our room, and that was what we did. Even Samantha seemed to know it was time and yawned, giving us the perfect out.

After a series of hugs, Samantha opened the portal, and we walked back into our dark room. Only when we stepped through did we see Jack, Lisa, and Apryl hiding in the corner. Samantha closed it as soon as we were through instead of letting it close on her own, as she usually did.

"What the hell took you guys so long?" asked Lisa, as she stomped out of the corner and over to my desk. There were three jars and two bowls sitting on it.

"You were invisible. How were we supposed to know when you were done?"

Lisa thought about that for a moment, and then suggested, "We probably should have come up with some kind of signal."

"You were invisible. What were you going to do? Wave an invisible hand in my direction?"

"Oh yeah," Lisa said, stumped.

"We could have dropped something," suggested Jack.

"You almost did," I pointed out. "Did you get everything?"

"Yep," Lisa pointed to the desk. "Everything's right here, including a bowl to mix it in, and..." she reached back inside the backpack and pulled out a roll of blank parchment paper. "Yep, we have everything except the last ingredient."

Everyone in the room knew what she meant and looked at Samantha.

"Are we going to do this now?" she asked.

"Yes," I said sternly, without explanation. When I saw both the concern and reluctance in her eyes, I took her hands in mine. "We need to. He needs our help and every moment we waste keeps him in danger. We can do this. Trust me on this. This will just show us where he is, and we can then develop a plan to go find him." I already had a plan. Once everyone was gone, I was going to go get him.

She agreed, reluctantly, and then held out a finger and I knew what she was offering. My first move was one of consultation, but not of the text. It was Apryl.

"You're supposed to be gone," I reminded her sternly.

"Not a chance. You may think you don't need me. You do. More than you know."

"Stop being dramatic, and just leave." I pointed to the door, but once I saw her shift her weight back on her heels and cross her arms, I knew it was settled and I had lost. She was as stubborn as they came, and I gave up, exacerbated. "You going to be okay with this?"

"Of course," she replied, dismissing the concern I had rather quickly, but that quickness bothered me. It seemed like nothing more than a reactive answer. I stared at her and searched her face and eyes for the true answer. I finally received it with a curt nod.

"Okay then." I looked at Lisa, and she glanced at the book on the table. There was nothing left to do but start. We walked together, nervously toward the book. I would be lying if I didn't say I felt some apprehension about this. This was next level magic. Even for me.

We arrived at the table, and I opened the book to the page. Lisa pulled out a piece of paper from the pocket of her long black coat. She opened it up and placed it on top of the page with the spell. "Congero," she said, and then began reading the instructions from her paper for everyone to hear as her finger traced each line.

"First, we put the drop of blood in the bowl. Then mix in two ground up sprigs of sage wood, two milligrams of silver dust, and a quarter cup of rose geranium infused vinegar. For every quarter cup of blood needed, we add a quarter cup of vinegar."

"Potion measurements need to be exact," I whispered, remembering Mrs. Tenderschott's daily warning before class began.

"Got that covered." Lisa rummaged through her backpack and pulled out a scale and measuring cup. "I came prepared." She sat both down on the desk.

"All right, Miss Girl Scout. If you are so prepared, how much do we need to make to cover that?" I pointed at the rolled-up piece of parchment. Lisa picked it up and then rolled it out onto the floor. It was a lot larger than I thought and seeing it didn't really help with the answer to the question. All I knew was we needed a lot.

"We could start with a quarter cup and then make more if we need it," suggested Lisa.

"No. We can't," I said defiantly. "That would require multiple samples from Sam. We won't prick her fingers more than once. We need to do this right the first time." I looked right at Lisa and saw her swallow hard.

"Okay, then," she studied the paper on the floor and then poured out one and a half cups of the vinegar and measured out six milligrams of the silver powder. Next, she pulled out six sprigs of sage wood and put them in a stone bowl. I knew where this was going. I had done it many times myself in Mrs. Tenderschott's class. We needed to grind the sprigs into a fine powder with a pestle. Getting it fine enough was the trick. Too coarse and it doesn't interact with the other ingredients, making the entire mixture off and the spell worthless. "While I do this," she looked right at me, "I need you to get the last ingredient."

I turned and looked at Samantha. She stood there, with a hand already held out for me. It shook. I took it and caressed it reassuringly before I selected a finger. Lisa, Miss Prepared, handed me a lancet and the bowl. I let go of Samantha's hand and held the bowl below it. Then spun the lancet in the fingers of my other hand and positioned the sharp edge just a breath's distance away from her finger. We locked eyes, and she answered the unasked question by pushing her finger slightly forward. I smelled it before I saw it. The first of several drops emerged and found their way to the bowl. It was intoxicating, but so was how brave my daughter was. I looked deep into her eyes and damned my own. She couldn't see the pride I had in her at that moment. Not that the finger prick was all that terrifying or torturous. It was how she took control of the situation. She knew what this was about and was as committed as I was to see it through. What I saw staring back at me started out as the face of my daughter, but then there were hints of another one. A look I hadn't seen on her face before, but one I knew well.

"Larissa!" cried Apryl, and I heard Jack start toward Apryl. "It's not me!"

I looked up at Samantha. Her eyes had turned black and shook as they searched for the source of the smell. I squeezed off the pinprick at the end of her finger and slammed the bowl back to Lisa. I didn't wait to feel her take it before I let it go. I hoped she was paying attention and grabbed it.

"Sam. Look at me," I said, taking her face in my hands. "You can do this. Just hold on and push it away. Fight that urge." Her head pulled back from me, but I held on. "You got to fight it."

"Samantha, listen to your mom," Apryl commanded. "I know this is hard. We both do. We have been there before. Fight it. Don't give in."

The smell diminished, and the blackness of her eyes followed suit. There was now a pungent odor in the room replacing that sweet metallic aroma. I pulled my daughter's face close to mine and caressed it. "Good girl."

"I covered it for now and poured the vinegar into the measuring cup. That should help until we produce the final quantity," Lisa said.

I turned around, still holding Samantha tightly. Her breath rushed in and out of her lungs at a sprinters pace, but it was slowing down, and I thought, *well, that answers that.*

Jack took over grinding the sage wood while Lisa spread out the parchment and readied everything else. She had it set up as an assembly line, and I could see she wanted to perform a quick mix and go right to the paper to avoid a repeat of what just happened as much as possible. She checked the contents of the stone bowl a few times, each time asking Jack to go finer. He never complained or objected. He just did as he was told until she finally said it was enough and took the bowl to its place in line.

"Ready?"

"Yep," I said, tightening my grip on Samantha, readying myself for a protest at how hard I was squeezing her.

We all watched as Lisa first combined the sage wood and silver powder. Then, as the instructions said, she added a half cup of the rose geranium infused vinegar for every half cup of blood we wanted to produce. So, a cup and a half. The odor was pungent to my nose. So much so, I barely noticed the smell of the three drops of blood in the bowl when she removed the cover. She didn't leave a big opening for that smell to escape before she poured in the mixture of the other contents over the top of the drops, and I breathed a sigh of relief.

"Are you ready for me to start the spell?" Lisa asked, holding the bowl.

"Let me do it," I volunteered. This was my mission, not hers.

Lisa held out the bowl for me to take, and the acidic vinegar odor invaded my nose before my hand grabbed it. I felt Samantha step back from my side, probably from the smell. Even Jack moved away. To save everyone from the assault, I stepped forward toward my desk where Lisa had prepared the potion, and then made an embarrassing discovery. Not only had I not asked Mr. Demius what the ingredients were earlier, I didn't even ask him what the spell was. "Um, I don't know it," I said with chagrin.

Lisa looked at me blankly.

"I never asked Mr. Demius about the ingredients or the spell. Just what it was."

I offered the bowl to Lisa, and she quickly took it. "Good thing I not only asked what it was, but I also practiced it with Ms. Tenderschott." She held the bowl in both hands, and quickly said, "Haec sume, fac plura. Haec sume, fac plura."

The contents bubbled and boiled to the top of the bowl's brim. The acidic vinegar smell dissipated, and the metallic smell of blood returned in force, turning the contents red. I turned and saw Samantha reacting again. Apryl wrapped her arms around her in a bear hug. "I got her. You finish this."

"The parchment."

Lisa was one step ahead of me and already had it spread out on the floor. She dribbled the contents of the bowl on the paper, and it soaked it up like a sponge. With no other way to spread it, we both began using our hands to spread the blood from edge to edge. It didn't take long to soak the material.

"Do the spell now."

Luckily, I knew that one, or knew where to find it. I sprang up from the floor and threw the paper containing the instructions for Congero up in the air, exposing the page I needed. It had both the Latin and English versions. I just imagined me butchering the pronunciation of the Latin words, so I opted for English.

"Blood is thicker than water, but runs like a river through our bonds, and keeps us always connected. Find Nathan Saxon and lead us to him."

The parchment shook against my floor. Then it spun around, slinging blood and sparks everywhere. I watched it and looked for any signs of a map forming in the blood., but nothing formed. Instead, the center of it disappeared before our eyes, with sparks forming around its edge, showering the room. Inside the sparks, I saw something appear. A place. Then I realized what this was. I made a quick check of the page, and realized I had read the wrong spell just as the ring of sparks engulfed the room, and all of us with it. Luckily for me, I had packed up the jars of my magic boosters in a bag and could grab it before it closed.

17

"I read the wrong spell."

"You what?" Lisa screamed, throwing her hands up in the air. Until that moment, everyone was looking around, exploring the forest that my mistake had landed them in, but once I made my admission, they were all looking at me in disbelief.

"The pages faced each other. There was one spell to produce a map, which was the one I wanted to read, but I accidentally read the other one."

"And what did that one do?" asked Apryl. "As if we don't know." She swiped at a bare branch on a nearby tree.

"Probably landed us in a random forest in the middle of nowhere," remarked Jack as he stomped through the underbrush.

"Mom?" Samantha asked, distressed. I held up a finger to put Apryl's question on pause while I rushed to my daughter.

"What is this line I see in front of me?"

"Line?" Lisa asked and joined me next to Samantha. "Did she ascend?"

I shook my head, no. I knew exactly what Samantha saw, and the others would have too if I had told them what the spell I read actually did. Now was the time to let them in on the secret that only I knew.

"That line is the path to your father. That is what the spell I read does. It takes you close to them and then leads you to them. The one I thought I was reading was supposed to draw a map to them." I ran a hand through my hair.

"Well, that's stupid. Why doesn't it take you right to them?" asked Jack. He stood next to Samantha and attempted to see the line himself. Of course he saw nothing and walked away shaking his head.

"This was not my plan. I wanted to create the map, and then come find him. On my own, and prepared. This wasn't how I wanted it to go at all," I sorrowfully apologized. "Lisa. Jack. I need you guys to take Samantha and Apryl back to the coven. Let me finish this on my own."

The two stubborn looks that responded were not surprising, but their presence was disappointing.

"Guys, this isn't the time to be obstinate."

"That's a word only an old person would use." chided Jack. "We aren't going anywhere, and, I seem to remember, you don't have the ability to send us back yourself." He twisted that last bit into my side with a smirk. He was right, but there was still someone that could, and she wouldn't tell me no.

I grabbed my daughter's hands and looked into her eyes. "Sam, this is something I need to do. Take the others back to the coven. I will return with your father once this is all done."

I felt her hands squeeze mine. This was her saying goodbye before she left with the others. I knew it and was about to thank her when she surprised me.

"No. I won't. You need us, and most of all, you need me. I can see the path to him. You can't, and don't you even think you can convince me to tell you where it goes."

Samantha let go of my hands and walked away, leaving me looking right at Apryl and Lisa. Never one to let a snide remark go unspoken, Apryl said, "Rebellious teenager." Then she and Lisa walked past me, following Samantha.

"Mom, are you coming?" Samantha called.

I was about to start one last protest to appeal to someone's, anyone's, sensibility, and logic, but I stopped. I knew good and well nothing I said was going to change things. My friends had already proven how stubborn they can be more than a few times, and Samantha, well, she was my daughter, and that told me everything I needed to know.

"I've got everyone's back," Jack said as he passed, joining the procession that now weaved through the woods behind me. He stopped just behind me and whispered, "But, just to be safe, you should load up." His hand tapped the bag of jars, causing two of them to clink together.

It was an excellent suggestion, and while he joined the rest of the group, I pulled out the half empty one and made it completely empty. After I put the empty back in with the others, I tossed the entire bag over my shoulder with its strap and rushed to the front of the line to walk next to Samantha. "Wait up."

She didn't. No one did, but I caught up to her quickly, and didn't waste the opportunity to admonish my little rebellious teen. "It's not wise to just go traipsing through the woods like this. If your father is here, it's a safe bet he isn't alone."

"Come on mom. I was raised around vampires. I think I can handle myself."

I admired her ego, but her naivety scared me. "Sam, what you were raised around were not vampires. They are friends who are vampires. Ones that have superb control. The ones you run into out here won't be like that. They will be vicious, and no matter how confident you feel as a witch, it won't matter. They will be on you before you know it."

I felt her glance in my direction as she continued to walk through the woods. I wish I could see what she did, but I didn't. All I saw ahead of us were dark woods with trees swaying in the wind above us. "So where are we—"

"What about my other side?" Samantha asked, interrupting my attempt to find out where the path took us. "Or are you going to avoid what happened back in the coven?"

"No, I don't guess we can." I threw my arm around her daughter. This was going to be our first big mother-daughter talk, and it wasn't what most mothers talk to their daughters about, boys. "I need to know what you felt when it happened?"

"A burning in my throat unlike anything I have ever felt."

"Ah yep. What about what could you hear or see?"

"Everything went out of focus except that feeling, and the smell." Samantha reached out in front of her and tensed up her fists. "Just thinking about it now. I can almost smell it. It makes me want to jump out of my skin and run."

"Yep, I know that feeling. What about now? What do you feel or hear?"

She let go of her tensed up fist and stretched her fingers out into the air in front of her. "Nothing, just the wind, the damp air of the night. A creak of a branch here and there when the trees move in the wind. That's it."

"You don't hear any thumping?" I asked.

"No, why?" she answered with a question, and turned to look at me.

"Because you have two witches walking behind you with beating hearts. You should be able to hear them."

"Oh," she said before turning to face forward, deep in thought. Or I assumed. That look could have been her trying to feel what I told her was there. After a few seconds of creaks and pops of the branches above us, Samantha asked, "Do you feel them?"

"Yep. I hear and feel every beat of their hearts." I glanced back and saw a very awkward expression on both of their faces. I imagine it was weird hearing a vampire talk about the sound of your own heartbeat.

"Jack sounds anxious," Apryl teased.

I didn't have to see Jack's eyes to know they rolled.

"I'm not sure why you can't hear them. I guess it's possible you have some abilities, but not others."

"Is that even possible?"

I didn't know how to respond to my daughter. Hell, I still didn't understand how I was possible. Could she have some vampire abilities, but not all of them? "I guess anything is possible."

There was a stifled giggle behind us. I turned to catch Lisa trying to hide it. I didn't see what was so funny, and she seemed rather embarrassed at being caught.

When I turned back, she said, "It makes sense. You were always a mystery. Why shouldn't your daughter be mysterious too?"

There was another giggle and chuckle at that comment, and I had to admit, I even had to hold back my laughter. It was true. Samantha appeared to be the only one who didn't get the joke and even appeared confused by it. "I'll explain later."

That did little to remove her confused look. If anything, it added to it, but we pressed on cautiously.

We resembled a war movie Mr. Bolden would have enjoyed. A few steps, and a stop if Apryl or I thought we heard or felt something. We were the ones best equipped for a stealth approach, so we took on the responsibility of being the lookouts. After we realized it was just a rabbit or fox working their way through the low brush themselves, we moved on.

To be honest, stumbling across the living wasn't my chief concern. It was stumbling across those like us. That was what I was worried about. We could walk right up to them, or they to us, and neither Apryl nor I would know they were there. They would probably be on us so fast we wouldn't be able to react. I only hoped they would be friendly, or what would be the best outcome, just Nathan. In and out, and back home. That would be the perfect outcome, but you'd think I'd learned my lesson about hoping for the simple route.

"I see the end of the path!" Samantha pointed off in the distance, and I saw it too. Not the actual path. Only Samantha could see that, but I saw what was at the end of it. It had to be it.

"I don't like this," whispered Apryl. Without me knowing it, she had moved up next to me.

"Me either."

Ahead of us in the dark dense fog stood a church time had forgotten. It stood there, looking gothic and haunted with crumbling walls and broken stained glass windows. There was what I guessed was some kind of overgrown walkway up to the cracked stone steps. A tree stood proudly up through the center of where its roof used to be. The scene was haunting enough, but what really bothered me was the silence. There was nothing around it. No animals, or anything, and I grabbed hold of Samantha's hand to yank her to a stop.

"What is it?" asked Jack.

"Nothing," I said. "That's the problem. Wait here." I had only taken a step, maybe part of a second one, before there was a quick flash of a portal behind me, several screams, and then a large thud sending me to the cold ground. Someone fell on top of me, and by the sound of the groan, it sounded like Apryl.

A quick push forced me up off the ground and sent Apryl flying off my back. I was up on my feet, ready to fight, before she landed behind me with a groan. The problem was whoever knocked us down was nowhere to be found. That was another problem. The biggest problem, Samantha, Jack, and Lisa, were missing too.

"Samantha!"

"Lisa!"

Nothing except the crickets singing the night away. I remembered the flash. "I thought I saw a portal. Lisa must have taken them back to the coven."

"Maybe," Apryl said as she marched around searching the darkness like I was. "I'm more concerned about who hit us." She stepped forward and stood aggressively. Her hands balled into fists by her sides. "Hey assholes! Try it again!"

I took up a similar stance and readied a little surprise in each hand for any visitors. There was no doubt they were out there. They had to be, and I heard a light rustling in the surrounding underbrush, but I didn't feel an animal.

"Come on out, and I won't kill you," I announced, hoping to encourage a nice, peaceful surrender.

"Not likely, you dirty witch," a voice responded from the darkness.

I sent a fireball toward the disembodied voice as my reply. It kept flying through the trees, illuminating everything it passed in a bright red hue, including the image of three figures running off carrying three other limp and familiar figures over their shoulders. I took off without a word to Apryl, but she must have seen it too. She was close on my heels.

"Let them go!" I cried, resisting the temptation of releasing a hell storm on them as we gave chase. The risk to our friends was too much. The figures carrying them were fast, but not as fast as we were. We weren't weighted down. We were gaining, and I was considering how to handle them once we were close enough. Taking a page out of Gwen's playbook and giving them a little telekinetic pull around the ankles to send them to the ground would be safe enough. I was about to pull it off too, when who I had to assume was the source of the disembodied reply popped up and knocked us down to the ground again.

This time, he didn't disappear like he had the first time. He stood there, over us. "Vampires consorting with witches. You have a lot of nerve." I pushed up, but then I felt a foot press down on my back, planting me on the ground.

"Stay down," bellowed a second voice from behind us. This one was deep, imposing, and hostile and obviously the owner of the foot that was pressing me down. I glanced ahead of us and saw the figures we chased getting further and further away, and I couldn't let that happen. I pushed again, and the foot pressed me down. Then I let loose a little surprise in the form of a telekinetic push and a nice enormous ball of blue flames straight up. The foot moved, and I was up, staring face to face at two vampires.

Both were male, maybe mid-thirties, and dressed rather modernly in jeans, shirt, and rather expensive looking sneakers, which were caked with the mud from our current surroundings. One was stouter than the other and wore a baseball hat backwards upon his head. Not at all like the ones from Jean's coven that were stuck in time two centuries ago.

They both looked me up and down, almost studied me. The stout one with the deep voice made the obvious observation, "You're a witch."

"Yep, I am." Then I sent them both flying through the woods. His baseball cap floated harmlessly to the ground in front of us.

I searched the darkness for the other figures and caught sight of them as they ducked into the dilapidated church. Nathan was in there. Or so the spell said. Now my daughter and friends were in there too, so that was where we were going, and we would not be covert about it either.

With an impressive flash, I blew the rotten wooden door to splinters and ran in.

"Put them down!" I ordered. It was unnecessary. They had already placed Samantha, Jack, and Lisa on the ground. They were still alive, but unconscious. My attention was so focused on them, I hadn't taken the time to survey the room. I wish I had. I was someone who just made a very dramatic witch like entrance and was now standing in the middle of vampire central. There must have been four or five dozen vampires in the room, and from the sound of chatter that had started, my presence was not welcome. Which was completely understandable, given the current circumstances. If that wasn't bad enough, the deterrents I held in each hand had lost a little of their luster, and somewhere I had lost the bag carrying my boosters.

"Larissa?" Apryl asked apprehensively.

It was probably because she was seeing something I had never done before. I was backing up. My steps backward grew in size once I lost the fireball in my left hand. I could feel the one in my right hand on life support. The horde of vampires now crowded around us, and I could no longer see Samantha and the others. The red glow in my hand faded out, and darkness engulfed us. Now it was the horde who was taking bigger steps.

"Maybe we should–"

I wasn't really sure what Apryl had in mind, but I was pretty sure it wasn't what I did. Her squeal proved that when I dropped both hands, let my fangs show, and leaped forward, grabbing the closest vampire and stretching its neck to the point of its the skin beginning to tear. "I'm here for Nathan Saxon! Where is he?"

The crowd gave room as I forced my unwilling partner forward. I had no intention of really removing the burden of his head. I just wanted to make a point. I was also a vampire, just like them.

"He's–" started a voice from the crowd, but the collapsing of the church under a great flash of purple and green muffled the answer.

18

Again, I found myself on the ground, and there was more than Apryl on top of me this time. Just to my side was the young man I had recruited moments before. He took one look at me, hopped up, and took off running. In fact, everyone scattered.

"Apryl!"

"Right here!" she screamed back. Then I felt a hand on my foot and spun around and up to my feet, offering her a hand to help her get up. Several of the scattering vampires smacked into us, sending both of us spinning like tops. When they cleared, Apryl grabbed my shoulders and spun me around once more, and then pointed. Lying on the ground were the others. Seems in all the commotion the vampires had forgotten all about their prisoners, and that was fine with me. I ran over, feeling great relief and ignoring the chaos that had just ensued.

I grabbed Samantha and offered to grab either Jack or Lisa. Apryl waved me off before throwing both of them over her shoulders and stepping right over the pile of rubble that was a wall a few moments ago. I followed, but then turned back to make one more check for Nathan. I didn't see him, but that didn't stop me from taking a second look. He had to be here. That spell led us right to him. There was another flash, sending a shower of crushed stone blocks over my head, and carried Samantha following Apryl into the trees.

Explosions of color from behind us illuminated the trees and the shapes of the vampires running through them. The rumbles followed us, closely. I grabbed Apryl and urged her to move faster. The splinters destroyed trees rained down on us. I made a few brave glances back to see if I could see what witch was responsible for this assault. When I saw a line of witches in dark cloaks walking toward us, I turned and pushed Apryl faster, causing a quick annoyed look and a huff from her. As soon as she spotted what I saw, she no longer had any question, and put the pedal to the metal. If we were a cartoon, there would be smoke coming off of our feet.

How long and far we ran until we couldn't hear the rumbles anymore, I didn't know. As far as I knew, we could have been miles away. We were also alone. There was no sign of any vampires, the line of witches, or the glow of the fires they started. I placed Samantha down on the ground and tried to wake her up. She had a scuff on her forehead but was still breathing. I pulled her head into my lap and caressed it, and begged for her to wake up, but she didn't. They had hit her pretty hard. I felt my body rock back and forth while I held her head. Rage was building inside, and while before I felt relief at not seeing the line of witches anymore, now I needed a target. Even some vampires would do.

Lisa was partially awake and complaining about Apryl's bony shoulder digging into her ribs. Jack moaned before rolling over and going back under. He seemed to suffer the worst with a large gash on the side of his head.

"What was that?" Apryl asked.

"Yea, what the hell was that?" Lisa groaned.

"Well, which time?" I snapped. "First it was vampires. They knocked you, Sam, and Jack out and took you to some old broken-down church. Then a group of witches arrived and blew the church to hell in a colorful attack."

"Oh crap. Sam!" Lisa crawled along the ground to Samantha's side, moaning in pain the whole way. She grabbed Samantha's hand and began rubbing it. "Come on, wake up." Then she looked up at me. "I should have taken her back when you asked me to. I'm so sorry."

"I thought you did."

"I tried, but... I don't know. I just remember opening a portal, then it all went black." Lisa rubbed across her face briefly and then reached back for Samantha's hand.

"I think she's okay. She's breathing." I had already tried a few times to pull the pain from her and help her wake up. A trick I learned from my mother after a rather clumsy period in my pre-teens that produced several skinned knees and elbows. She said it was a mother's touch. I had tried it once on my own when I was probably fifteen to pull the sting out of a bee sting, and it worked. It wasn't working now, but I was sure that was because I was out of juice.

"Lisa, can you help her? Please?" I pleaded, and then, feeling completely helpless, I said, "I can't."

"I think so." Lisa moved up next to Samantha's head and sat opposite me. She looked as if she wanted me to lay Samantha's head in her lap, but there wasn't a chance in hell I was going to let go of her. Lisa was just going to have to maneuver closer, and that was what she did until she was practically hovering over Samantha's head with a concerned look.

Lisa extended out her hand and let her fingers drape lightly across Samantha's forehead. She closed her eyes, and I watched as a white glow escaped between her fingers. It pulsated, like a heartbeat, and then stopped. Samantha groaned and turned her head.

"Ouch!" she screamed and tried to sit up.

"Don't," whispered Lisa. "Just lay there for a bit." When she removed her hand, that large scrape that had been there before was gone.

"Mom?" Samantha asked, looking up at me with glassy eyes.

"Stay still," I suggested with my voice, and then again with a light rub on her forehead. "I guess, my darling, you aren't full vampire."

There was a chuckle from the lump of flesh that resembled Jack. "I never thought there would be a time I was actually jealous of you guys." He ended it with a groan.

I looked around again, and both saw and felt no one around us, but there was still a tremor of rage inside, and I asked Apryl to see if she felt anyone. She didn't. "Let's rest here for a bit." It wasn't like we had a choice. Three of us were in no shape to go anywhere, and to be honest, I didn't know where to go. We followed the spell, and the attack interrupted us before we found Nathan. Where he was now was again a mystery. So close, but yet again, so far.

Jack and Lisa pulled themselves up against a tree. I was going to give them another few minutes to recover before I asked either of them to open a portal and take us all home. I didn't see that we had any other choice. Then it started. Probably because my mind was no longer thinking of plans to find Nathan, and there was now an empty spot it could slide into. When it slipped in, it pushed other things around to make room for a huge heap of regret for what had happened to my daughter, and even my friends, all because of some foolhardy plan I had, yet again.

I couldn't do this to them or myself anymore. I knew I should have listened to Mrs. Saxon and all the others who said things would work out if I just let them. Here I was, trying to rush it. I was trying to put things on the timetable I wanted, and as usual, it backfired. From this point forward, no more. I was going to just let things happen. Let things follow life's plan, no matter how slow it was, or how long it took. The only question I really had left was, could I do that?

"Are you the one asking about Nathan Saxon?"

I never heard the approach of the jeans and denim jacket wearing young vampire that bounded into the center of our recovery spot. Why would I? Most wouldn't hear me coming, either. He stood there, weary, ready to run, as Jack and Lisa jerked back and crawled up the tree to help them get to their feet. Apryl was already up, but she didn't seem that concerned. Just a little shocked, which was a look Samantha, and I both shared.

"Are you the ones asking about Nathan Saxon?" the young vampire asked again, this time impatiently, as he looked at each of us, ready to bolt.

I helped Samantha up to a seated position against the tree behind me and stood up. I looked down apologetically for jostling her such. My eagerness to respond caused me to move a little fast. That eagerness hadn't tempered any when I stepped toward our visitor. I was there next to him in an instant. "Yes. I was asking about Nathan Saxon. Do you know where he is?" I asked cautiously, trying to put up a dam against the wave of hope that threatened to wash over me.

"You're not here to hurt him, are you?" he asked, looking at Lisa and Jack grimly.

I grabbed him by the chin and turned his head to look right at me. "No," I said while shaking my head, slowly, with a lot of concentration going into the slow part. "We're family. We know his mother, and he is my boyfriend."

He looked around at us again before the tension in his face melted away. "Follow me."

I was about to ask him to slow up, anticipating he would sprint off, but he seemed more mindful of who was in our group and their current state. He even offered to help Jack and Lisa to their feet. Samantha could walk, but barely. I threw her arm over my shoulder and helped carry some of her burden. Her injuries were my fault. With everyone ready, he took the lead and didn't say another word. He just walked.

We silently followed our mysterious guest through the dark forest for what felt like hours, moving through the trees, and avoiding any roads or paths. With the cloudy skies above blocking the moon, it was hard to tell if we were moving north, south, east, or west. All I was certain of was we were heading in a straight line deeper into the forest, which became thicker with every step.

Behind me, I heard Jack and Lisa stumbling from time to time. Probably over a downed tree, or thick brush. In this darkness, they wouldn't see them. To me and Apryl, it was as bright as daytime. I watched Samantha and saw her step around or over obstacles on the ground and crossed that vampire ability off the list.

After what sounded like a very painful trip, Lisa asked, "Can I use light? Just a little glow..." Our escort flashed right in front of her face, and shock choked off her words.

"Do you want witches to find us?" he asked intensely, and without waiting for an answer, he continued. "You do? Don't you? Shine a little beacon so they can find us." The man was seething under his whisper.

"No–" Lisa attempted to answer, but again he cut her off with a finger right in her face.

"Maybe this was all a setup. I heard his mother is a witch. You all arrived just before the attack."

"Whoa, wait," Apryl whispered urgently, and she shoved her arm between him and Lisa, pushing him back a few steps. She took the opening to step in between them. "You can stop right there."

But he didn't. All he did was change the target of what sounded like pent up aggression. "Why are you defending them? You're a vampire god dammit. Do you know what they are?" His voice lost a little of its whisper before he caught it and backed the volume down to just above a breath.

"Yes, I do. They are my friends. So is Nathan, and that is why I am here. That is why they are here. We aren't part of this stupid war. Do you have a problem?" And very Apryl like, she didn't give him a chance to answer her question. "If you did, why did you come find us? Huh?"

"I didn't know they were with you." The words burst from his lips in a ferocious whisper. He looked right at Jack and Lisa, and I felt it was time to take some of the heat off of them.

"But you knew I was there, and I'm a witch too."

He looked at me, confused. I could almost see him replaying the image of me bursting through the door, ready to unleash hellfire.

"Me too," added Samantha.

My eyes cut in her direction, and I mouthed, "leave it." I knew what she was trying to do, but I didn't know this vampire, and I didn't know his intentions. If he attacked the witches in our group, she was in no shape to defend herself. None of them were.

"Don't you see?" I asked, hoping to find some rational thought inside his head buried in that mountain of anger and hatred. "We aren't like the witches that have attacked you. We are actually against all this, and just want to help our friend. Now, will you take us to him?"

For the briefest of moments, I saw "no" in his expression, but he turned around and kept walking in the direction we were originally heading.

19

For the next two hours, we marched forward with Apryl guiding Lisa and Jack every step of the way. I found a little humor in the bickering that ensued each time Apryl missed something they needed to be told to avoid. Each instance didn't last long. They were just momentary accusations that she was doing it on purpose. It was mostly from Jack. Lisa sounded more accepting and understanding, saying that while Apryl may have seen it, she didn't think it was large enough to be a problem. I only intervened once. I asked Apryl to put herself in their shoes. How would she like to be walking around out here with a blindfold on, and not able to see anything at all? I think she got my point as the amount and frequency of direction coming from her for them to step over something increased.

The feeling of being watched was neither a witch nor a vampire ability. It's something that was very human, and one of the creepiest sensations to experience. It's even worse when you multiply that by a hundred. That was how many sets of eyes I felt were watching us as we walked. I reached over and grabbed Samantha's hand, and pulled her closer. It was good timing too. Something to our side just moved through the low underbrush.

I heard a protest from behind, followed by Apryl shushing it. I glanced back. She had Jack and Lisa walking very close together in front of her. Her own head twisting from side to side at the sounds. Our escort had to hear the same sounds we did, but he never flinched. Instead, he just kept on walking, and I took that as a sign. He knew what was out there, and he wasn't concerned. That didn't stop me from being defensive and pulling Samantha even closer still.

He walked right up to a tall bush and paused a moment, and glanced back at us. His expression had something to it. I couldn't quite put my finger on what it was, but it set me on edge, and I pulled Samantha completely behind me and crouched. He pushed aside the tall bush and exposed a small clearing with dozens of other vampires standing or sitting. Others emerged from the woods as we stepped through. Each of them continued to eye us curiously, and I knew why.

My grip tightened on Samantha's hand, and she didn't mind. She tightened her grip even more and pulled herself closer to me. This crowd was an eclectic gathering of vampires. Every age range, gender, and race were represented, as well were the clothing styles of the last century. There was a large portion in more modern attire, and a few that appeared to be stuck in the 60's. The ones that had my attention were the ones toward the back of the group that were still dressed for a time that I remembered well. Our escort weaved us through the crowd, right to them.

The stares intensified when we approached them. I recognized some of their faces from New Orleans, but I couldn't put a name to them. It was clear they all recognized us. A few stepped in our way and wouldn't move when our escort tried to push through, and that appeared to be enough for him. He turned around, shrugged, and walked off, leaving us there, now surrounded. It was a moment of déjà vu for me. I had been in the same situation the last time I went back to bring Nathan home. Then we retreated. Now we didn't have that option. We were outnumbered, outgunned, and surrounded. Even if I had my crap together, it wouldn't have made much difference.

"We don't need to do this, do we? We are just here to find and help Nathan Saxon." I said, trying not to sound too much like I was pleading, but I was. They didn't seem to accept it, and a large section of the horde seemed to lean toward us. I whipped around. "Lisa, get them home!"

"Larissa! Larissa!" cried a voice from heaven. It froze me in my tracks and froze Lisa.

Frances Rundle pushed through the crowd and grabbed my hand. "Come with me!" She yanked me and Samantha through the crowd. I glanced back and made sure the others were following close behind.

Frances led us through a group of vampires to another clearing among the trees. There were more vampires there, but not nearly as many as where we had just left. As each of their heads spun in our direction, I watched as they parted like the Red Sea. Inside, Fred Harvey leaned over another vampire on the ground. Just by the looks on everyone's face, I didn't need anyone to tell me who that was, and I ran to him and collapsed next to him.

A felt a hand on my shoulder and looked up at its source. "He's burned on the outside, but healing," reported Fred Harvey. "Magic burns worse than fire."

I looked down at Nathan. He lay there motionless, with patches of charred skin covering him. I reached over and gently touched an unscarred area, and Nathan groaned. I wanted to throw my body over his and use my body to soak up his pain, but I knew that wouldn't work. He groaned louder as I gripped his hand. Every touch caused him pain.

"It's magic burns." Lisa kneeled down and looked him over. "It's still there too."

Now it was my turn to groan. I had hoped it was dissipating and he would be better soon, but as I looked up at his face, that chiseled thing of Greek gods, the charring continued to grow. He wasn't over the hump yet.

"Can you neutralize it?" I asked, as if some kind of chemical had caused this.

Lisa shook her head with a dark expression. "Yes, but not here. It takes a potion, spread over his skin."

I kept my focus on his eyes. Waiting for them to open, just as I had up in my bedroom when he first turned. They weren't opening, but he was busy behind the closed lids. "Let's get him home."

"Absolutely," said Lisa as she stood, and I gathered Nathan in my arms to pick him up. He screamed as I lifted his body off the ground and turned.

Samantha stood there, staring at her father for the first time. I wanted to tell her this wasn't what he normally looked like. The Nathan I knew was full of life, laughter, and love. His personality alone could chase away all the darkness in the world, and God knows, there is enough darkness out there. Without his light, the darkness felt heavier. That weight may have been what caused a quiver in Samantha's lips.

"He's going to be fine," I said to calm her, but inside I felt I needed a bit of convincing myself. Nathan felt like a dead weight in my arms and looked like a corpse burned to a crisp. The only signs of life were his moans, and the constant shifting of his eyes behind his eyelids, and his painful moans.

"Can you send back some of that potion?" asked Fred Harvey. The request caught both Lisa and me off guard, and we turned back to him. He was standing there, literally hat in hand. "There are lots just like him. Every attack is the same. Barrages of large, colorful blasts. Those caught in the flash end up like him. They suffer for days, sometimes a week or more. Some haven't recovered completely."

Lisa looked at me. I was just as surprised by the request as she was. Here, in the middle of all this, a vampire was asking a witch for help. I felt it was the least we could do, and gave her a quick and eager nod, and then gave our answer to Fred. "Of course. We will make as much as we can and send it back. Just as soon as we get back."

The ground beneath my feet thrusted up with enough force to toss me back against the closest tree. I held on to Nathan tightly and attempted to protect him when we landed. It was not a graceful one, and I fell on my back like a turtle holding him. Then it happened again. The sound of the great cataclysm caught up with the heaving of the ground and, in the bright flash, I saw the shadows of vampires flying. I didn't see them land before I did, but I had to assume most landed around the same time I did based on the collective groaning that filled the air.

Still holding on to Nathan like his life was my life, I stood up and looked around for the others, and I saw them. Not far away. Apryl was brushing herself off while Jack, Lisa, and Samantha appeared to land a little more gracefully. They probably used magic to aid their flight.

What I saw approaching behind them proved to me that magic was the reason we were all sent flying. That column of hooded witches had caught up with us. Behind them, the remnants of magic scarred lands that most mortal eyes wouldn't recognize. I saw it. There was a glow in the air, and the lines of the universe were fractured.

I ran carrying Nathan and screamed at Lisa. "Open it! Now." Then another blast hit between us, sending me tumbling backward. Nathan's body flew limp over my head. I tried to grab him, but missed before we both hit the ground, stunned. There was a loud ringing in my ears and a burning sensation on my back. With every attempt to rise, I was forcefully shoved down and disoriented by the loud ringing in my ears. I didn't know which was up or down. I knew Nathan was laying a few feet to my right, but that was all I was certain about and I was only sure of that because I could feel him with my right hand.

"Samantha? Lisa?" I cried out as loud as I could, but I couldn't even hear it myself over the ringing, yet alone their answer, if they answered.

My fingers gripped at the ground, trying to pull myself out from under the weight that had me pinned down. One hand crawling, the other hand dragging Nathan, but it didn't matter. The weight followed me and stayed seated right in the center of my back with every movement. My plan to fight as a vampire wasn't working. The witches weren't fighting fair, but why was I surprised? I fought the same way against Jean and his followers just a few months ago.

"Lisa? Jack? Can either of you do anything?" I screamed, in hopes they could fight magic with magic, but again I couldn't hear myself over the loud ringing. I clawed again at the ground. Needles burned through me, and my fingers turned to bones as they dug into the dirt. My skin was nothing but translucent paper. Then the weight lifted from my body, and I levitated a few inches off the ground. I hung there, just out of reach of the blades of grass that attempted to stand back up. My blood charm dangled from my neck and rested on the ground. My body then slowly rolled. I kicked and moved my arms, but nothing stopped me from rolling away from Nathan. I lost sight of him, and another face came into view, and my blood boiled. Seeing the charm that dangled from her neck explained everything.

"Now Larissa. What are we going to do with you?" sniped Miss Sarah Julia Roberts from beneath the hood she quickly pushed off, revealing her long blonde hair.

"Let me up, and you will find out."

"That's not going to happen," she tilted her hand, and I tilted up with it. "We don't understand how you escaped Mordin, but we will find out, and find out who helped you," she said with conceited confidence that grated on me. "We won't make that mistake again." She turned her attention to Nathan. "How painful the Fires of Ruel are. He will feel that pain for an eternity. Only a witch can counteract it. It's one of my favorite spells taught to me by my mother, but I bet you don't know that spell." She leaned in closer, and the effects of the charm dug deeper. "You don't know a lot of things, and you will never be my supreme," she sniped with a nasty sneer.

The hatred I felt for her caused my arms to jerk, and to both of our surprise, they almost broke free.

"Oh," she said, feigning surprise after she had recovered from her real startle. "We know all about your little plan to challenge. You just need to give up now. There is no way you could pass the seven wonders. You aren't a strong enough witch."

"Like I said. Let me out of here and let's find out." I shouted back, and again my arms jerked free. This time enough to reach out and grab her skinny throat. I ignored the tearing of my paper-thin skin as my fingers squeezed. The pleasurable feeling of her gasping for air made it all worth it. I felt my hatred for her flow through my arm, forcing my hand to squeeze even tighter. I hated her, not because of what she said about me never being her supreme. I didn't give a rat's ass about that at the moment. This hatred was all about what she had done to Nathan, and not to mention how she had treated me before.

In the distance, I saw the others held similarly by other witches. Samantha struggled against her magical bonds. Apryl was sprawled out on the ground and looked like a skeleton. Lisa and Jack appeared more complacent, which I found oddly curious, but that was something to ponder after I took care of Miss goody-two-shoes-witch. As much disdain as I felt for Gwen, she was still an angel compared to Miss Roberts. I squeezed a little more and felt her heart hammering all the way up the arteries in her neck. It matched the fear I saw in her eyes. I could easily finish the job right here and right now. Then, in the distance, the witch that had subdued the others raised her hand and threw me back to the ground. Miss Roberts' throat was ripped from my hand. Red scratches left by my fingernails marred her milky flesh.

She collapsed to the ground, gasping for air as the mysterious witch walked by her, leading the others away. "Stop playing with her and bring her."

20

This was an unpleasant déjà vu on so many levels. Frozen, floating, and frustrated to the point of wanting to kill the first person I got my hands on. I actually had that chance, but I didn't follow through. I could have squeezed just a little harder until her windpipe popped. That's not a sound I had heard before, but I imagined Miss Roberts' would have produced a glorious pop. The look on the face of the owner of said windpipe would probably have been even better

Lisa, Jack, and Samantha walked on their own. Well, they walked. I can't really say it was on their own. They appeared to be zombies that just followed this mysterious new witch. Neither appeared to be harmed more than they already were. That was good for our captors. If someone even made a scratch on them by having them walk too close to a tree branch, they would suffer more than a scratch. I figured I could remove the burden of a head from two, make that three witches before they stopped me. It was tempting to find out, especially since I had regained some movement in my hands , but I needed to wait for my opportunity.

We came to a small cottage nestled between the trees. It wasn't anything special, but it wasn't run down. The mysterious witch entered first, and then Nathan and I were taken inside. I could now move both hands and my lower arms, but that still left me helpless as I watched Samantha and the others disappear further into the woods. I lost sight of them when the door closed behind us. There was no surprise to find us some place other than the inside of a small cottage.

We were in a place right out of some medieval fairytale. Old wood floors and stone walls with fluted columns held up grand archways. Large, aged metal doors lead to the next room and to the outside where we came from. I heard its loud clang when it closed behind us. Dark, rich wood pieces of furniture were everywhere, with the pièce de résistance sitting on a platform right in front of us. A throne with spikes adorning the top of it worthy of having families fight over.

There was no surprise at seeing the mysterious witch walk up to it and have a seat. Her hood still obstructed the view of her face. Seeing Miss Sarah Julia Roberts step to her right side tipped me off, though. It had to be Mrs. Wintercrest, our supreme. Oddly, I never see her as one that would be out here doing her own dirty work. She seemed the type that would have others that were eager to prove their loyalty to go out and serve as cannon fodder.

"Mrs. Wintercrest. I'm the one you want. Help Nathan and send him back home." I threw myself at her mercy, or more offered myself as a sacrifice. Helping Nathan was first, the others were second, and I figured I could take care of myself if I needed to. What was she going to do? Send me back to Mordin?

"Hush, child," the mysterious woman said. Her unfamiliar voice echoed in the stone room. "You are right in that you are the one we want, but I am not Mrs. Wintercrest." She sat up straight on the edge of the throne and reached up with both of her ring adorned hands and pushed back the hood, revealing a much older version of Miss Sarah Roberts. "I can see how one might make that mistake. The throne and all. But that just shows your narrow view of the world. As you can see, I am not her, but as you can also see, I don't need to be to have more control than she ever will. She is just a puppet that serves me well."

"So, you're the real supreme?" I asked, confused, with my head spinning. "And you're her mother?" I looked at Miss Roberts, hoping the answer to that question would not be a yes. Miss Sarah Roberts stepped away from the throne and strolled around me and Nathan. My body convulsed as she passed with that charm. She even leaned down a little lower.

"Again, such a narrow view of the world. I expected more from someone from your family, Larissa. Mrs. Wintercrest is just who you see, but if you look below the surface. She is a shell of a witch. Her power has long left her. We are the ones propping her up for special benefits in return." She held out a hand toward her daughter, and Miss Robers bowed.

"So, she can be supreme," I whispered as the realization hit me. Then it all made sense. What I had observed before in the coven. Finding her leading the attack in New Orleans. Even how she responded and treated me when we first met.

"They always said you were a bright witch there, Larissa. Yes, that favor, among others," she continued. "The Council of Mages used to be a hallowed institution. It was comprised of the greatest families of our world. Each family had a seat. Each family ruled with dignity and strength. We were not ones to be defied or challenged. The vampires knew that. Everyone knew that. But, one by one, the houses have died off, allowing other, undeserving families to take their place. Each weakening the council's strength. We are going to set that right and restore the council to what it should be. An order that is not to be messed with. We just didn't know that at our weakest, fate would present us with the greatest of opportunities. A trifecta of sorts," she giggled with a nod to her daughter. Miss Roberts had her normal smug look on her face as she made another pass around me. The pain and searing I felt from her charm made me regret my show of restraint earlier.

"An opportunity to eliminate two troublesome families, the Dubois and the Meridian, much of the rogue witches, and the threat of the vampires all at once. It was too good to pass up. We just didn't plan for you and Marcus to be as slippery as you are, but fate," she paused and looked down at Nathan's limp body and smirked, "has brought you back. Marcus won't stay hidden for long. He doesn't have it in him. Then all the threats will be eliminated, and my daughter, not you, will ascend to supreme. Leaving one great family ruling over the council."

So that was it. That was why Miss Roberts was hellbent on making my life miserable from day one, focused on trying to have me exiled, and why she always seemed right at Mrs. Wintercrest's side, almost pulling her strings. I should have seen it before now. I always knew it was because they considered me a threat, and I thought I understood why. but I was wrong, so horribly wrong. None of that mattered now. Nothing mattered except the person lying beside me, groaning in pain, and my daughter wherever she was.

"Do what you want with me, but help him, and let my," I paused before I said daughter. Telling her there was an heir to the Dubois line was signing a death sentence for Samantha. "Let my friends go."

"The witches will be processed and repatriated once we know they aren't a threat. The vampires, including your beloved there, will be disposed of," she coldly announced.

"Disposed of swiftly," added her daughter with such satisfaction and glee in her voice, it made my insides boil.

"No! They are not a threat. Nathan's mother is a witch. He will not be a problem. Let him go back home!"

Miss Roberts stopped and hovered over Nathan. "The only safe vampire is a dead vampire." She held her hand over him. She had removed her charm and now held it just above Nathan. His body writhed.

"Stop!" I jerked my hands free from their current frozen state and lunged at her. She was out of reach. I lunged again, thinking I could drag my entire body closer, but I didn't move. Each attempt added to the size of the smile across Miss Roberts' face.

"Stop! Kill me!" A flood of tears joined my screams.

Her smile grew at that suggestion, but she never paused to even consider that possibility. I was ready to die. I would die a million times over to stop his suffering. The tears continued as my hands balled into fists. I pounded the air in front of me, hoping to connect with her just once. If I could get my hands on her just once, I wouldn't make the mistake I did earlier, and it would be quick. She taunted me the whole time, even taking a step closer. She was close enough that the air created by my swipes sent ripples through her robe, which she noticed and waved it at me tauntingly. All that ended when I felt a pulse of rage surge through me, and there was a flash, sending Miss Roberts across the room and into a stone archway. I felt it surging through me, with my anger and rage. It was back. Me. I was back. My magic was fully back. Mr. Demius may have been right. My emotions power me, and this was rage.

With a quick yank, I pulled the charms away from both witches, popping the chain from around their necks.. I crushed them into a powder in the middle of the room and then sent a hurricane gust to blow it and the two witches that wore them against the wall.

I threw a pentagram-based rune at Nathan for protection against what had happened, and anything that was going to happen, from this point forward. I saw the universe clearly, and the lines wrapped around him tightly and arched out a way to deflect any incoming attacks. This was working.

Next, I shot a barrage of fire at Miss Roberts' mother, aiming at her head. She attempted to move out of the way, but I yanked on the lines that surrounded her and pulled her back. She countered with a fast push that hit me before I saw it, and then she ducked before the balls of blue flame reached her. They crashed into the wall behind her.

Now it was my turn to return the favor, and I sent a push in her direction. She tumbled at first, but I watched as the lines around her straightened out and she landed gracefully on the floor. I was about to follow with another stern shove and a wide spray of fire, followed by opening up a hole under where she was going to land. I figured that would be something she couldn't counter, and probably wouldn't see coming. It would have been grand to carry it out, but her daughter countered with something of her own, sending me flailing into the wall behind me. I felt her magic burn, but with a single motion, I pushed it off of me and attempted to send it back where it came from. It hit her on the leg, and she went down to one knee.

Her mother hit me again, with something small, but it stung worse than anything I had ever felt, and it caused me to double over before I fell to the ground on my knees. I felt a strange draining sensation, but that didn't stop me from sending a shot back her way, that finally caught her off guard, and sent her flipping head over heels. Here we were, three witches giving our best to kill each other. I considered it a rather futile activity, being that I couldn't die, but that didn't mean it didn't hurt like crazy. Mrs. Roberts hit me again with her stinger which arrived with a trail of fire and sparkles, and it again sent me to the ground. That crap hurt, and if I made it out of here, I was going to need to learn how to do it myself.

It was two on one, but I was holding my own. I delivered two telekinetic pushes, one with each hand, sending both of the Roberts sliding across the floor. It bought me enough time to open a portal back to my room in the coven. With another telekinetic shove, I sent Nathan sliding across the floor towards it, but just as he reached it, a flash pushed him to its side, and closed the portal. Before I could see which of the two did it, another burning flash sent me back to the floor. So far it seemed I had spent more time on my knees than I had standing up.

Nathan groaned loudly. He was coming to and now his body could register the pain more. I threw variations of the pentagram at him as fast as I could, surrounding him in glowing symbols burned into the wood floor. That would protect him. At least for a little while. I think I stood there and admired my glowing handiwork for too long. A burning sensation in my back sent me down to my knees yet again. It almost laid me out flat, but I forced through it as hard as I could to stay upright to defend Nathan and myself. The impacts were coming fast and hard from behind. With everything I had, I turned to see Miss Roberts stalking toward me, closer and closer, with every round she leveled at me. I tried to retaliate or defend myself, but another impact interrupted each attempt.

Miss Sarah Roberts cackled when I was finally sprawled out on the floor under the weight of each of her attacks. She picked up the pace and walked closer. That was her mistake. While I wasn't able to respond as a witch, she forgot what else I was. A quick swipe of my hand knocked her to the ground. I was on her before she even breathed. A primal instinct inside me caused my body to lurch down with my fangs out, targeting her neck. I was inches away before I realized what I was doing and stopped. There was no way I was going to give her that gift, but that didn't mean I could use my fangs to rip a few vital arteries so I could watch her bleed out. I leaned in to feast, but her mother hit me with a rather powerful blast from behind. It attempted to pick me up off of her daughter, but there was no way I was letting go of her this time. I reached down and grabbed her by the throat and pulled her up with me. She dangled from my grasp as I leered at her mother. I was holding her daughter, but technically, she was the one who had her life in her hands. The longer she held me there, the longer her daughter would hang there, kicking, struggling to breathe. Each gasp I felt her throat make added to my leer. The panicked thumping of her pulse was music to my ears.

Her mother didn't release me. She held me right there, high above the floor among the arches, with her daughter kicking in my grasp below. Her mother squeezed me, just as I was squeezing her daughter. The only difference was, she kept her distance. From the safety of across the room, she mumbled something and then a blinding blue light hit me, and I felt my flesh burn.

I tried to throw rune after rune to protect myself, but the pain forced each image out of my head before I could put it to work. The same with any spells I could conjure, or even opening a portal. It was all-consuming. So much so, my grasp on Miss Sarah Roberts' slender throat slipped, but even if it was my last act in this world, I wasn't about to let her go free. With a quick squeeze and a very toothy grin through the pain, I accomplished what I wanted, and then tossed her aside like a rag doll.

Her mother shrieked and dropped me to the floor. I landed, and my body instantly recoiled into the fetal position from the burning. I shivered and shouted, waiting for her next attack. Then I felt an arm over me and looked up to see Nathan slinging his body over me. Inside I screamed—NO! He was not doing this again. I pushed him away and I forced my body over his, while doing my best to look at Mrs. Roberts as she hovered over her daughter's limp body. How I wanted to spring to my feet and do the same to her, but my body was in no shape to cooperate. It was all I could do to throw myself across Nathan to guard him from any more suffering. A question flashed through my head about who would protect him after she killed me, but I ignored that as I did what I could to cover every inch of Nathan. It didn't help that he was a good foot taller than me.

I made another feeble attempt at opening a portal, and watched as it sparked open, but then it disappeared with another flash of blue that now engulfed both Nathan and me. The pain shot through me like a hot iron, burning both inside and outside.

"You will both die for that," she cried, and then did it again, and I knew she was right about our fate. I again tried to open a portal. Escape was our only option, and that was a fleeting one at that. Sparks flew, and it opened, just as another flash arrived, and my hand dropped and clutched at my chest. The portal didn't close. It opened wider, and then a large flash came through it, planting Mrs. Roberts into the stone wall behind her. Samantha and Apryl stepped forward. Apryl stood guard hissing, with fangs displayed. Blood dripped from her hands. Without a word, Samantha swiped her hand, throwing Nathan and me through the portal.

21

It would have been great if my daughter had put us back in our room, but it was possible something distracted her when she threw us through the portal. They say timing is everything. Well, timing wasn't on our side. We landed in the middle of the grand entry between both staircases just as the Council of Mages walked through. Our presence was just a momentary distraction. The real show was occurring through the portal. The sounds of a horrible battle with screams and wails leached through. I looked back through it, as did everyone else.

Apryl was doing her best to sink her teeth into Mrs. Roberts, but continued to come up short, while Samantha bombarded her with all Master Thomas had taught her. She was throwing everything at her. Fireballs. Spells. Lightning strikes. She even threw her through a wall. It wasn't more than a few moments before Mrs. Roberts reappeared. I wasn't sure how to pull that off. I even watched in surprise as Samantha gave up on her magic and opted for a more physical approach, and teamed up with Apryl. Samantha went low, and Apryl went high with blurring speed, taking Mrs. Roberts off her feet. Apryl grabbed her by the shoulders and yanked her down into her throne.

"Burn the witch Sam," Apryl yelled.

Next to me, I felt Nathan reach out for me, and I met his hand halfway, and pulled him close. His body was still burning, and I looked up to the council for help. None of them were paying any attention to us at the moment. They were focused on the battle on the other side of the spinning disk.

Samantha followed Apryl's lead. Instead of falling back on how I would have done it, she spoke several words we couldn't hear over Apryl's chant of "Burn the witch. Burn the witch." A column of flames erupted from the floor and consumed the throne. Apryl leaped back just in time. It burned for several seconds, then the flames bowed out and disappeared. Mrs. Roberts sat on the throne, untouched, with a glow only I could see around her.

The large metal door they brought us through sprang open and several more witches ran in.

"Apryl! Samantha!" I called and got up to my feet. They heard me and sprinted for the portal. Apryl had to leap over Miss Roberts' body on her way out. It was the first time any of the council had seen her, and it produced several gasps. The portal closed with Samantha and Apryl safely through.

Not fully understanding who we were dealing with, I threw up several runes that etched themselves into the walls and doors of the coven. There were no combinations this time. Just simple runes to lock the place down and block any attempts to follow us. Mrs. Saxon had done the same once upon a time to keep me in. I broke through. I could only hope they wouldn't be able to do the same.

"What is the meaning of this?" demanded Mrs. Wintercrest.

"Who are you to be giving orders?" Apryl asked as she stalked around the council, keeping her distance because of the charms they wore. Something that I quickly remedied, removing the charm from each member of the council, and sending them through my own portal to some place I didn't really care where. All I knew was it was far away from here.

"You," Mrs. Wintercrest pointed right at me. "You are exiled again to Mordin, and this time you won't be able to escape."

"Just hold your horses there, grandma," sniped Apryl, who stopped and glared right into Mrs. Wintercrest's eyes.

The commotion in the entry had drawn an audience up and down the stairs, and a murmur had developed. I could hear many of the questions being uttered by those surprised to see me. Others were concerned for Nathan, and I heard Mike forcing his way through the others that lined the stairs to get down to him. Kevin Bolden was on his heels. There was another presence that created quite the murmur. "Who was the new witch?"

There was banging on the door to the girls' side of the vampire floor, and Jennifer Bolden looked at it with great suspicion, but still opened the door. Jack and Lisa came running out and down the stairs. "Damn charmed doors," uttered Jack.

"Mrs. Wintercrest, I don't believe you are in any position to be giving any orders." The effects of the war I had just been through dripped away, and every ounce of my abilities returned. It was then I saw something that Mrs. Roberts had alluded to. She was absolutely right. Mrs. Wintercrest was weak. Why hadn't I seen it before? Then I knew. I hadn't been around her much since I knew how to read the magic in the universe, and when I had, Miss Roberts was right by her side.

"I'm... I'm... your supreme," Mrs. Wintercrest responded, all flustered. Her cheeks turned red, and as she huffed, ready to explode.

"Yes, that is the title you hold, but not what you are. Isn't that true?" I took a cue from Apryl and stalked around her and the council.

"Now wait a minute," said one member of the council. One of the Mr. Demius lookalikes that I was never formally introduced to. He stepped forward to intervene, but Mr. Nevers grabbed his arm.

"Do they know?" I asked, staring right at her as I circled around her. Her head attempted to follow me as far as it could before she had to turn her entire body.

"Does anyone here know?" I asked loudly. My voice echoed in the rafters. I studied the faces of the council members intently, hoping to catch a hint of familiarity or comprehension in their eyes. There it was. A glimpse at a few of them.

"What is going on here? Larissa!" exclaimed Mrs. Saxon as she entered the hall. Mike stood up from where he and Kevin Bolden tended to Nathan. "Nathan!" She ran to her son, falling to his side. "Oh, Nathan!"

Lisa joined them. "It's the Fire of Ruel."

"The potion!" Mrs. Saxon blurted. She looked around. "Mike. Kevin. Help, get him up and follow me."

She jumped up and headed for the other hallway. I had to assume it was Mrs. Tenderschott's classroom. Whatever they would need for the potion would be in there.

"Rebecca, you need to stay here and control your witch!" Mrs. Stephanie Morrison cried out, which I found odd, but maybe it wasn't. She was one of the few that I saw a glimpse of recognition in.

I knew Nathan needed help. That was something I knew better than anyone, but I also needed Mrs. Saxon to hear this. I was torn. Two needs. Which would outweigh the other? I remember an old movie, something Mr. Norton watched. Well, maybe it wasn't that old. The needs of the many outweigh the needs of the few. As much as it pained me to delay Nathan's help, that was what I had to do.

"Lisa! Go with them!" I ordered. "Tell Mrs. Tenderschott what she needs to do. Mrs. Saxon, I need you to hear something."

She stopped dead in her tracks and looked back reluctantly. There were tears running down her face. That was the first time I had ever seen that kind of emotion from her, but I understood. I would be there too if I wasn't so pissed off.

"I can help too," Gwen, the princess of pink, called from the witch's landing.

"No," ordered Mrs. Saxon as she choked back her emotions.

"Who here knows that a witch named Mrs. Robers, the mother of Miss Sarah Julia Roberts, has been propping up and pulling the strings of Mrs. Wintercrest for years?" I didn't wait for an answer. "Who here knows that her daughter was being groomed to replace Mrs. Wintercrest? That will never happen now. She is dead." There was a gasp up and down the stairs behind me. "Who here knows that Mrs. Wintercrest has lost most of her power as a witch, and has been relying on that family for support for years? And... that family is the one running this war to remove the last remaining powerful families in our world, mine and the Meridians, while also eliminating the rogue witches and vampires?"

I looked around at the stunned faces. "I'm going to guess," I stopped my circling of the council and walked right up to Mrs. Wintercrest. "I guess no one knew that last part."

"I am still your supreme," she spat back, as defiant as ever.

"No, you're not," I replied with the same level of defiance and walked away showing her my back as I did.

"Is any of this true?" Mrs. Saxon asked.

"No. Of course not," denied Mrs. Wintercrest, but just as fast as she entered her denial, another answer emerged.

"Yes."

First it was Mr. Davis who stepped forward, then Mrs. Okina, who even stepped forward out of the shadows of the other council members and pushed back the hood of her red robe. In all my previous dealings with the council, she never once spoke up, and even now, she seemed afraid to. She had a reason to be concerned or even scared. She was speaking up against the witch she believed was the most powerful witch in our world.

"I don't know about their involvement in the war, but it doesn't surprise me to hear what you said. I know about Sarah and her mother. Sarah was to be the next supreme. She spoke of it often, reminding us of how important her family was, and how we needed to be loyal to them." She looked down at the floor, and her voice shriveled. "I am only here because I pledged my allegiance to them."

"It's just a damn blood feud. That is all this is," mumbled another member of the council. This claim created quite a commotion among them.

"Council members? Council members?" Mrs. Wintercrest attempted to restore order, but the damage had been done. Even how they all looked at her had changed. Their respectful reverence was gone. In its place were scowls. No matter how many times she called them, the commotion and conversations continued. She had lost all control.

"Council members!" Master Thomas called as he descended the stairs. His voice achieved what Mrs. Wintercrest's had failed. "We can all agree these are rather shocking claims. Why don't we disburse with the speculation and do a hearing of fact?" He stepped off the bottom step and toward the council, but before he joined, he walked over and whispered into my ear. "I have this. You go to Nathan."

And that is what I did. I grabbed Samantha's hand, ran down the hallway. Mrs. Saxon and Apryl followed us. I heard the council members start up a conversation again, this time with Master Thomas leading. I could only imagine Mrs. Wintercrest standing there, wilting away. It warmed, but also chilled me at the same time.

***

Again, Nathan stayed unconscious in his bed for several days, and again I sat there as a vigil. I think this was the third time. Twice here and once in New Orleans. This was not something I wanted to make a habit of. The potion that Mrs. Tenderschott whipped up did its thing. It wasn't something he had to drink. It was a lotion we had to coat the burns with several times a day, which I handled religiously. Samantha offered to help several times, but I reminded her this was my responsibility. It was what I caused, and I needed to fix it. She told me I was being obstinate, and I asked her where she learned such a big word. Rarely did she leave my side, while I tended to Nathan. She even slept in there. Being there when he woke up was important to her, or necessary, as she reminded me more than once. It was something I couldn't disagree with, though I wasn't exactly sure how to handle that introduction, or better yet, when. Was it something I should spring on him as soon as he woke up? Probably not, but as my new attitude dictated, we would cross that bridge when we came to it.

I left his side once on the second day for just a few minutes to apologize to Mrs. Saxon for going against her wishes, and prepared myself for a large lecture about how bad things could have gone, but it never came. Even when she asked me to sit next to her on her stark white couch. Even after she sighed and looked up at me. What she said shocked me on so many levels.

"Larissa, you did what I thought you would, but not what I had hoped. I have to realize you have your own path to follow, and I shouldn't stand in your way. Without you, I wouldn't have my son back. I owe you a great gratitude for that." Then she hugged me. I returned it cautiously while I waited for the but that never arrived.

Neither of us spoke another word about it during my vigils. It was not for lack of opportunity. She spent just about as much time watching and tending to Nathan as I did. And, we weren't avoiding talking to each other either. We spoke. We actually spoke more than we ever had. I told her stories about my childhood and my parents. She was extremely interested in my father's journals. I showed her a few combined runes, just some basic safe ones. I felt there were a few entries in my father's journals she would really find interesting and had Edward retrieve them for me. The council's original rules regarding my father's journals restricted their removal from the library. Edward made an exception in my case, stating that the world was changing, and they were my family's property, so he felt those rules didn't apply to me. So, I guess I have gone from rule breaker to the person who the rules don't apply to.

By the end of the second day, the bluish scars on Nathan's skin had faded, and his periods of consciousness had increased. At first it was just periods of moaning and groaning, and then one time he asked, "how bad is it?" He didn't stay awake for the answer.

By the end of the third day, his eyes opened, and as much as I missed his old eyes, I was over the moon to see those empty black orbs staring up at me.

"So, am I dead?" he asked with a bit of a moan.

"No. Worse. You are human again."

"Seriously?" he shot up and propped himself up on his arms.

"Nah," I shook my head. "You're still a vampire."

He thought for a moment. "I'm not sure which is better. I liked being human, but I like knowing I am going to be around with you forever."

"Um, about that forever thing," I started, and he looked at me curiously, and then pushed himself up further and sat back against the headboard of his bed.

"Changing your mind?"

"No. It's not that. You need to understand the rules of this immortal thing. It just means you won't die. It doesn't mean you can't be killed. I just wanted to clarify that part of being a vampire for you. You have put yourself in some pretty precarious situations so far, and you have only been one of us for about two months. Keep it up, and your forever may only be six months."

"Worried?" he asked, almost laughing.

"This isn't a laughing matter. And no, I'm not worried because I am going to be here to keep you from doing anything stupid ever again."

"So, you are going to be my protector?" he asked, leaning toward me, grinning.

I leaned in to meet him. "Absolutely. Someone has to," I whispered, and then kissed him.

"Good. I think I can deal with that," he agreed before he grabbed my head with both hands and pulled me in for another kiss. When he released me, he looked over my shoulder into corner of the room at the occupant that had gone unnoticed by him until then.

"If you're my protector. It looks like you have one too. Who is the new witch who saved your ass?" he whispered into my ear.

"It's a long story." Samantha scooted her chair up next to me.

Nathan jerked back against his headboard with a bang. I don't believe he thought she could hear his question with how low he whispered it.

I reached over and grabbed his hand and prepared myself. "Well, here it goes."

Up Next - Coven Cove Book 7—The Revenge of the Shadow Witch

1

"Mom! This is so unfair!"

Samantha marched out of my room and down the hall. All I could do at this point was be thankful we finally had separate rooms. Not that I didn't enjoy rooming with my daughter. I loved it. It made us closer than ever. In fact, we were probably too close in so many ways, especially now. I guess I needed to follow her.

"What is she calling us? Ugly?" Apryl asked. Her head poked through her cracked open door.

"Just ignore her. She's a teenager," I said, as I passed.

Pamela was standing in the hall and seemed to enjoy this for some odd reason. As was Marie Norton, but I understood that. It was a stepparent's payback, and I was sure my mother was going to tell me the same thing, if life slowed down long enough for me to make that trip back to see her.

"Look Sam." The door slammed in my face. She didn't lock it. We already went through that phase a few days ago, when we both realized we knew how to open doors without a key. A simple spell any young witch that is snooping around for

Christmas or birthday gifts learns. Mrs. Saxon taught it to Samantha as a kind of revenge, or let's call it a grandmother spoiling her granddaughter. I opened it and walked in. "I already told you there are two ways to handle it. Which way you chose is up to you, and you don't have to do anything at all."

Samantha sat at her make-up table, looking at herself in a mirror. She tried her hair up, then her hair down. Then she pulled it back behind her head in a ponytail. That was a particular look I liked. It took a few years off of her, which I was all for. There was something about your daughter looking just as old as you were that I just couldn't get past. The good news was she had stopped aging. So, we were forever stuck together, looking like sisters instead of mother and daughter. Something that more than a few made sure they pointed out, and a few of them paid for it dearly. We now know what sound Mike makes being thrown off the top of the coven. Fortunately, he landed on his feet. Unfortunately, that was probably where the good news ended, if you asked Samantha.

"It doesn't matter what I do," she cried.

"Yes, it does. You have two options." I looked into the mirror at her, and smiled, hoping how uncomfortable what I was about to say made me feel didn't leach through. It did. "Really, you have three options."

"Mom! That isn't even funny," she protested to my suggestion, and reached down and slid her tray of make-up closer to her. She eyed the compact of powder and foundation, and then picked up the compact for a moment before she dropped it back to the table. "There isn't enough of this stuff in the world to cover this."

"Then you have the other option."

"Magic?" she complained, looking up at me.

"Yes. Magic."

She huffed, rolled her eyes, and got up from her chair and marched over to the closet. "No way, Jose. That is so fake. I can't believe you ever did that." Without touching the handle, she opened the doors, showing the wide assortment of styles she had in her wardrobe. She and I were different when it came to this. I was a jeans and t-shirt girl, with a color palette that leaned heavily toward the blacks and grays. Samantha had skirts, dresses, tops, and pants of every color of the rainbow. "Maybe if I wear something more in your style, I won't look that bad. Now I understand why we are portrayed how we are in the movies." She slid half her wardrobe from one side of the closet to the other. The metal hangers made a terrible screech that sent chills up my spine.

I heard a knock on the door frame and hoped a savior had come to save me. "What's wrong with her?" Amy came waltzing into her room. Probably returning from an outing with Laura, which explained how she got past the charmed doors.

"Your sister is having a bad day," I said.

Samantha turned and looked at Amy with a disgusted face, sticking her tongue and fangs out. "That's what. And mom, try life. This is life. Remember."

I was about to remind her that this life would never end, so she better just buckle up and get used to it, but I felt that might light another fuse.

"Why doesn't she just do magic like you did for the Christmas party?"

"Because I'm not my mom," snapped Samantha.

"Don't snap at her."

"Sorry," Samantha acquiesced. "Sorry Amy. Want to come help me pick something out that will make me less ugly?"

"Yes, but you're not ugly," responded Amy.

Samantha just rolled her eyes and began pulling out outfits that comprised all gray, but leave it to Amy to pull out pinks and purples.

"How about these?" she asked.

"Oh sure. Those will just accentuate my ugliness," Samantha said, dismissing the suggestion.

"It will also make you look like a Gwen wanna be," Apryl added from the door.

"Stop," I warned her, and she held up her hand defensively, but had an evil smile on her face.

"Gwen's not all that bad," announced Samantha, and that caused the room to go quiet. Even Amy looked back at Apryl and me with a disapproving look on her face.

"Now that will get your mouth washed out, young lady."

"Sam, I don't know what you are so upset about. You have the best of both worlds." Apryl walked in and stopped to pose in the full-length mirror on the open closet door. "You have eternal youth. Your mom's good looks. That red hair that is to die for-"

"And I look like a ghost," interrupted Samantha. "Just a week ago, I looked like I was alive. Rosy-red cheeks and everything. Now look at me. Night of the living dead." She stiffened up her shoulders and rocked side to side, and even played like she was going to try to grab Amy, which produced a squeal.

"You didn't let me continue. You still have your eyes. Ask your mom, or any female vampire up here, what keeping our eyes would mean to us."

Samantha looked at Apryl like she was going to respond, but then stopped and continued her search for the perfect outfit.

"Sam, she's right. I would give anything for them. When I use magic to adjust my appearance, it is more for the eyes than anything. Our black eyes look so blank, and emotionless. You still have yours."

Samantha stopped her search for a moment to pull the closet door closed enough for her to look at herself in the mirror. "But they aren't even mine," she bemoaned staring at her own reflection.

It happened as soon as we returned. What the trigger was, I didn't know. It had to be something that happened, or how she tapped into some of her vampire skills when fighting Mrs. Roberts. It was the only explanation that made sense, especially since it was later that day that life drained out of her skin, leaving her just as pale as the rest of us. Her only saving grace, that we were all jealous of, were her eyes. She was not cursed with the empty black orbs the rest of us were. Instead, she had human looking eyes. A pupil in the middle of the ocean of white, but instead of her big blue eyes, they were now a deep and brilliant gold, like the sunset. She hated it every time I compared them to that. I could only hope that in time she would grow to appreciate them.

"I love your eyes." Amy looked up at Samantha beaming, sporting her own pair of yellow eyes.

"Ugh!" Samantha turned around. "Knock that off, and just be yourself, please."

Amy turned and looked at me, sporting exact copies of what Samantha's eyes looked like and a huge smile.

"Knock it off," I mouthed back. I almost needed to give the same warning to the giggling vampires behind me.

"Hurry up and pick something. We can't be late." I headed to the door, hoping if we were out of her hair, she might actually decide on something and get dressed.

"Yes, I know, mother," she practically seethed at me.

Amy handed her a shirt and a pair of jeans. "Here." It was something more like what I would pick, with maybe a touch of more color. The shade of purple of the top was a little light for my taste, but acceptable, and what I felt was a fair compromise.

"Fine!" Samantha declared, almost defeated. With a quick shove from behind, she ushered Amy out of the room, along with the rest of us.

"Nice pick." I gave Amy a high five before pulling her close and jostling her hair. Something she hated and hastily put it back in to place.

"Why doesn't she just use magic like you?" Amy asked.

"She thinks it being fake," I said with a shrug.

"That's silly."

I couldn't agree more, but that didn't move things along. "That's your older sister. She's silly."

"Yes, she is."

"Have fun with your witchy stuff today," Apryl commented as she walked away, waving over her shoulder at us. "I'm heading up to the deck for the day. It's nice and overcast." She turned around, and walked backwards toward her room and commented, "I could get used to this no class thing." Then she spun around and disappeared through her door.

"More?" whined Amy.

I nodded. "I'm afraid so. We'll drop you off on your floor on the way."

Samantha's door burst open with a whack, and she emerged in the outfit Amy had picked. She didn't wait for us, and just headed to the door, announcing, "I'm ready," when she was halfway there. Amy and I picked up the rear and followed. It was all we could do. Samantha wasn't waiting for us.

Out the door we went, and my heart melted at the sight on the other landing. There he stood, waiting for us, like he had done every day since his return. Nathan stood there, leaning forward against the banister.

"Hey dad." Samantha waved as she headed down the stairs. The perfect image of the American brooding teenager. She didn't stop or really look in his direction.

"Morning Sam. How's my beautiful daughter today?"

"Ha!"

All I could do was shrug and smirk. He returned the same.

"Hey Nathan," screamed Amy. I saw Samantha's back crawl at the sound of the high-pitched scream.

"Hey there, cutie. Are we still on for more board games later?"

Amy nodded, and then added. "You're going to lose." For a while I knew he was letting her win, but recently he confessed she had gotten him a few times all on her own.

Nathan didn't bother greeting us at the bottom of the stairs, or walking with us. He wasn't permitted where we were going. In fact, no one other witches were. And even though things had changed here in this coven, it was still better if vampires weren't even close to our destination.

I dropped Amy off at her floor and then followed my sulking daughter down the stairs and down the hall toward the classrooms. It was just us now. The normally busy halls with people rushing to morning classes were a thing of the past. They had canceled formal classes. We were mostly in a lockdown state. We still had access to the pool deck, which was protected, but that was it. No one was allowed in or out, and that included witches. Only a few exceptions were made, and Mrs. Saxon had complete control over that. She said this was how it had to be and it was just temporary. I couldn't see an end in sight, and that had nothing to do with my divination skills. She enlisted my help with the runes to lock down the coven, noting that mine were more powerful and lasted longer than hers. With everything I had put the woman through, I didn't hesitate. It didn't hurt that she practically guilted me into it by saying if anyone was going to break through them, it would be me, so why not just let me put my own up so it would be easier to get out.

We locked down the pool deck and a little area around the edge of the woods, knowing we needed to allow for some kind of outside exposure to fend off cabin fever. Of course, it wasn't like we were locked in a prison. This wasn't Mordin. This was an enchanted coven that created whatever your mind could create. If you really wanted to be outside, all you had to do was think about it and the room adjusted to make you think you were.

To secure everything the best we could, I used the same type of runes I had used to hold Jean and his followers at bay. I just added a few things to it for a longer staying pattern, but that didn't mean I didn't go out at first light every day to check and redo them to keep them in place. The only exception to my runes were the werewolves. They could come and go as they pleased, which had two purposes. One that they enjoyed, and one that they did out of obligation. They still ran checks night and day of the surrounding property for any intruders, just as they had before. The only difference now is they weren't just looking for the local drunk that had stumbled into a place they shouldn't be. They were looking for signs of witches or others approaching. The second reason was more of a compromise and suggested by Martin. Vampires had to feed, but we couldn't leave. It wasn't safe. So, it had to be brought to us, which was one reason for securing a small area at the edge of the woods. Martin and his brothers would chase small game into that area, letting us feed. Martin's original idea was for him and his brothers to kill it and drag it to us, but that took the hunt out of it for us.

We walked up to Mr. Helms' classroom and Samantha threw open the door, sending the occupants into a stunned silence.

"What? What are you looking at?" Samantha asked, standing there in the door's opening with her hands ready to go. When no one responded, she walked over and took her seat. Lisa looked back at me, concerned, and I wiped my hand down my face and pointed at my eyes.

Lisa nodded. She knew what was going on. Most of them in the room did. They had... make that most of them had tried to convince Samantha she was beautiful this way. One hadn't, and that pink princess eyed me the entire time I walked to my seat next to my daughter. This wasn't going to be a fun day.

Continue reading at the links below:
For the US Store, tap here.
UK, tap here.
Canada, tap here.
Australia, tap here.
Everywhere else, tap here.

Stay in Touch

Dear Reader,

Thank you for taking a chance to read this book. I hope you enjoyed it. If you did, I'd be more than grateful if you could leave a review on Amazon (even if it is just a rating and a sentence or two). Every review makes a difference to an author and helps other readers discover the book. Also recommend this to your family and friends that enjoy similar books, and if you are active on TikTok post a review there using the tag #CovenCoveSeries.

To stay up to date on everything in the Coven Cove world, click here to join my mailing list and I will send you a **free bonus chapter** from "The Secret of the Blood Charm".

As always, thank you for reading,

David

A big thank you to my beta reading team. Without all your feedback, books like this one would not be possible. Thank you for all your hard work.

Bloodwars © 2023 by David Clark. All Rights Reserved.
All rights reserved. No part of this book may be reproduced in any form or by any electronic or mechanical means including information storage and retrieval systems, without permission in writing from the author. The only exception is by a reviewer, who may quote short excerpts in a review.

This book is a work of fiction. Names, characters, places, and incidents either are products of the author's imagination or are used fictitiously. Any resemblance to actual persons, living or dead, events, or locales is entirely coincidental.

David Clark
Visit my website at www.authordavidclark.com

Printed in the United States of America

First Printing: July 2023
Frightening Future Publishing